BROTHER

and other stories

Further titles by Clifford D. Simak
published by Severn House

WHERE THE EVIL DWELLS
THE COSMIC ENGINEERS
THE MARATHON PHOTOGRAPH
SO BRIGHT THE VISION
HIGHWAY TO ETERNITY

BROTHER

and other stories

by

CLIFFORD D. SIMAK

SEVERN HOUSE PUBLISHERS

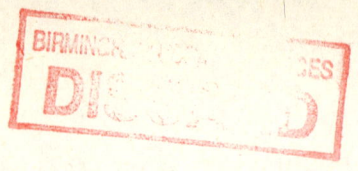

The first world edition published in 1986 by
SEVERN HOUSE PUBLISHERS LTD of 4 Brook Street,
London W1Y 1AA

British Library Cataloguing in Publication Data
Simak, Clifford D.
Brother and other stories.
I. Title   II. Lyall, Francis
813'.54[F]   PS3537.I54
ISBN 0-7278-1417-6

Printed and bound in Great Britain
at the University Printing House, Oxford

Introduction

Clifford D Simak is famous for the warmth of his tales, for the extent to which ordinary individuals and traditional moral values are the key to what happens, and for his ability to couch the strange in the ordinary and the familiar.

He started writing SF in 1931, and became one of those who supplied John D Campbell with the stories which made *Astounding Science Fiction* (later *Analog*) famous. But *Astounding* was not his only forum. Other editors were keen to see his by-line in their magazines. In the 1950's his novels began to show CDS's ability to weave a story of longer proportions than the then usual SF format, but he has also continued to write at shorter lengths. The tally of published work to date is more than respectable for a full-time author, and an extraordinary feat by a part-timer, albeit a professional part-timer. And the quality of that work, much of it accomplished in evenings after a normal day's work, is also extraordinarily high. His three Hugo's, a Nebula, a Locus, the Nebula Grand Master award of 1977, and an International Fantasy Award, to say nothing of a plethora of nominations, show the appreciation he is held in by both the SF readership and his fellow writers.

As he freely acknowledges, the spur in many of CDS's stories and novels has been his early years. Again and again throughout his long career in SF CDS has returned in creative imagination to the farms and bluff country which form the north-west corner of Grant County, bounded as it is on the west by the Mississippi and on the north by the last few miles of the Wisconsin. The stories in this collection show that clearly.

We met in 1981. CDS agreed to my visiting him in Minneapolis when I took a week-end off during a research trip to the United States. As a relaxation from some dessicating and detailed research into pollution law in Scotland I had the previous winter started to write about his fiction. As preparation I had therefore read all the CDS novels and short stories in my collection, in that of a senior programmer of our university computer, and also others provided for me by the Science Fiction Foundation of the North East London Polytechnic. Reading CDS in bulk was an interesting experience. The stories stood up well to that test, (not many other authors would), and I had questions about recurrent themes, names and locales. That, at least was one good reason for my asking to meet CDS. The other reason was simply that over the years his stories had given me so much pleasure that I wanted to meet their author. He seemed to be kin, like-minded, valuing the same sorts of thing. I was not disappointed. We spent a fascinating day together. Thereafter I drove down to Grant County and spent a couple of days exploring, mindful of what we had spoken about. His childhood friend, Oscar Ellis, (who died in 1985), was then still living on a neighbouring farm, and he kindly took me to see the actual farms of CDS's birth and growing up. I can therefore testify from experience that the feeling of place, and the values and characters the stories contain, is fully explicable when you have once looked over the rolling, gullied landscape to the south of the Wisconsin, and seen the steep bluffs falling north to the river. But even if you have not had that privilege, these stories transmit a great and good gentle strength, a strength like that of their setting, ancient and mellow.

Stories like those here enlarge and enrich the imagination and the feelings. They entertain not merely for the moment, but linger in the memory.

Brother is a remarkable story. I challenged CDS about it, and he replied that it was not written by any conscious wish to construct such a story. The elements in it which parallel his own life were a surprise to him when I pointed them out. Simply, it is a tale of twins. One has remained here on Earth, while the other has roamed the stars. Yet, as the story comes to its conclusion, see the actual relationship of these 'brothers'. CDS has been called by many the 'pastoral poet of science fiction'. According to Anderson, Lambert is 'the pastoral spokesman of the century'. Like many CDS characters Lambert sits in his rocking chair, and looks out over the farm where he was born and grew up. He sees the fireflies and hears the creek gurgling its way down to the Wisconsin. He knows his farm, its paths and byways. He knows of its secrets – but not all of them. No man born could know that. His talk with Hopkins is of farm matters, and of the swamp beast down at Millville. And he finally settles down with his 'brother' to talk beside the fire of that incident out in the Coonskin system. This is a cameo of a writer who has in mind roamed the stars, and yet who has remained among the whippoorwills, and the shouting russets and golds of fall amid the oaks and the maples on Military Ridge and Campbell Ridge (the two run into each other) of Millville Township, Grant County, Wisconsin. In sum, it is an unconscious self-portrait of the author. 'He had, he told himself, the best of two worlds' – how true.

'Over The River And Through The Woods' is the other purely 'Grant County' story in this collection. As in 'Brother' there is that acute writing of the farm which can come only when memory is an equal spur with invention. The first goldenrods are blooming and the wild asters are large in bud. It is apple-canning time, and the Mason jars are ready. There is the wood stove and wood box, the butter churn and the ticking clock. And there are other elements here as well. I have written of the craftsmanship of the stories: see the profound effect of one little detail in 'Over the River . . .' – Ellen Forbes's reaction to zips. Then again there is a personal touch, counterpointing the memory of the farm. Ellen Wiseman (née Parker) was CDS's maternal grandmother. He has paid elliptic tribute to her in other stories, notably in 'The Whistling Well' (in *The Marathon Photograph*, 1986). Here it is very clear that the grandmother who welcomes Paul and Ellen to that well-kept farm has a close relation to the author. Last, would you be surprised to know that CDS was once a stamp collector? Or as he would put it now, a stamp accumulator.

'Auk House' is one of CDS's excellent time track/ alternate world stories, and an addition to his 'houses'. CDS has written of memorable houses before, where the house is in effect a character in the story, Webster House in *City*, and Whitney House in *A Choice of Gods* being but two from novels. Auk House is also more than just a place in this story. It has a defined 'personality' of its own. The story itself is another contribution to a theme which CDS has tackled several times, that of the person manipulated by others, but in ways which turn out to be for good, whether or not the manipulators so desire, a theme which is as old as that of Joseph and his brothers in Genesis. This story, like 'The Whistling Well' referred to above, also raises the possibility of an intelligent dinosaur species, and its ethics and religion, together with the further possibility of mutual recognition by sentient species. Echoing other Simak thoughts, it also suggests that somewhere there may be monitors, policemen, or referees, watching to see that the human race does not make a mess of things, watching to see when we may be wise enough and fit for entry to the paradise worlds. And all these intriguing speculations are apart from such throwaway ideas as whether a sense of outrage is needed for philosophy!

Two other matters: first, while Auk House is not of this world, and we are told that Latimer was driving on a county highway near the coast, we are also told that he was making for Wyalusing. Wyalusing is the name of the bluff to the south of the confluence of the Wisconsin and the Mississippi, and lies but a little west of Military Ridge where the Simak farm lies. We are therefore not far from the locale of 'Brother' and 'Over the River and through the Trees', for the Mississippi itself is like a sea at that point. Second, note what happens to Latimer. He starts the story rather depressed and down. At the end he is happily content and about to be enfolded in company he desires. He has gone through perils to the rosy glow of what, in 'On Fairy Stories', J R R Tolkien called the eucatastrophe, that reversal which in fairy stories makes all prior privations worth-while. Once again in a Simak story someone who has pressed through and has stuck to his principles and traditional values, although under great pressure to abandon them, receives fulfilment. Lambert, who has recognized the worth of alien intelligence, is rewarded for his perception.

Last there is one of my most favorite Simak tales; favorite both because of what it is, and also for sentimental reasons. I encountered it in the first SF hardback I ever bought, away back in 1956, when hardbacks were something to be bought with care and much consideration, and rarely were fiction. 'Kindergarten' contains many of the CDS elements spoken of above. The setting is clearly the bluff country of CDS's youth. There is the threatened tragedy of Peter

Chaye's cancer which has sent him running to that land.
There is the clean caring of Mary. There is the coming of
the alien, and the gift of the jade. There is the reaction of
blinkered authority. There is the promise of the Teacher
for those who can benefit. There is trepidation and yet
the glad acceptance of what that benefit will mean.
There is the open-endedness of the tale – it has no
conclusion in anything other than the technical sense
and we are left to dream on. In short, there is a fusion of
traditional morality, of compassion and of delight in the
promise of all coming to a true fruition. This story therefore encapsulates all CDS's power and the attractions
which have made him one of the Grand Masters of SF.
Fifty-five years he has been writing, delighting
generations of readers. And the story-well which he has
tapped is by no means exhausted. Another novel, *Highway to Eternity*, is published in Summer 1986. We are
glad.

Aberdeen, Scotland   F Lyall
April 1986

Brother

He was sitting in his rocking chair on the stone-flagged patio when the car pulled off the road and stopped outside his gate. A stranger got out of it, unlatched the gate and came up the walk. The man coming up the walk was old – not as old, judged the man in the rocking chair, as he was, but old. White hair blowing in the wind and a slow, almost imperceptible, shuffle in his gait.

The man stopped before him. 'You are Edward Lambert?' he asked. Lambert nodded. 'I am Theodore Anderson,' said the man. 'From Madison. From the university.'

Lambert indicated the other rocker on the patio. 'Please sit down,' he said. 'You are far from home.'

Anderson chuckled. 'Not too far. A hundred miles or so.'

'To me, that's far,' said Lambert. 'In all my life I've never been more than twenty miles away. The spaceport across the river is as far as I've ever been.'

'You visit the port quite often?'

'At one time, I did. In my younger days. Not recently. From here, where I sit, I can see the ships come in and leave.'

'You sit and watch for them?'

'Once I did. Not now. I still see them now and then. I no longer watch for them.'

'You have a brother, I understand, who is out in space.'

7

'Yes, Phil. Phil is the wanderer of the family. There were just the two of us. Identical twins.'

'You see him now and then? I mean, he comes back to visit.'

'Occasionally. Three or four times, that is all. But not in recent years. The last time he was home was twenty years ago. He was always in a hurry. He could only stay a day or two. He had great tales to tell.'

'But you, yourself, stayed home. Twenty miles, you said, the farthest you've ever been away.'

'There was a time,' said Lambert, 'when I wanted to go with him. But I couldn't. We were born late in our parents' life. They were old when we were still young. Someone had to stay here with them. And after they were gone, I found I couldn't leave. These hills, these woods, the streams had become too much a part of me.'

Anderson nodded. 'I can understand that. It is reflected in your writing. You became the pastoral spokesman of the century. I am quoting others, but certainly you know that.'

Lambert grunted. 'Nature writing. At one time, it was in the great American tradition. When I first started writing it, fifty years ago, it had gone out of style. No one understood it, no one wanted it. No one saw the need for it. But now it's back again. Every damn fool who can manage to put three words together is writing it again.'

'But none as well as you.'

'I've been at it longer. I have more practice doing it.'

'Now,' said Anderson, 'there is greater need of it. A reminder of a heritage that we almost lost.'

'Perhaps,' said Lambert.

'To get back to your brother. . . .'

'A moment, please,' said Lambert. 'You have been asking me a lot of questions. No preliminaries. No easy build up. None of the usual conversational amenities. You simply came barging in and began asking questions.

You tell me your name and that you are from the university, but that is all. For the record, Mr Anderson, please tell me what you are.'

'I am sorry,' said Anderson. 'I'll admit to little tact, despite the fact that is one of the basics of my profession. I should know its value. I'm with the psychology department and. . . .'

'Psychology?'

'Yes, psychology.'

'I would have thought,' said Lambert, 'that you were in English or, perhaps, ecology or some subject dealing with the environment. How come a psychologist would drop by to talk with a nature writer?'

'Please bear with me,' Anderson pleaded. 'I went at this all wrong. Let us start again. I came, really, to talk about your brother.'

'What about my brother? How could you know about him? Folks hereabouts know, but no one else. In my writings, I have never mentioned him.'

'I spent a week last summer at a fishing camp only a few miles from here. I heard about him then.'

'And some of those you talked with told you I never had a brother.'

'That is it, exactly. You see, I have this study I have been working on for the last five years. . . .'

'I don't know how the story ever got started,' said Lambert, 'that I never had a brother. I have paid no attention to it, and I don't see why you. . . .'

'Mr Lambert,' said Anderson, 'please pardon me. I've checked the birth records at the county seat and the census. . . .'

'I can remember it,' said Lambert, 'as if it were only yesterday, the day my brother left. We were working in the barn, there across the road. The barn is no longer used now and, as you can see, has fallen in upon itself. But then it was used. My father farmed the meadow over there that runs along the creek. That land grew, still would grow if someone used it, the most beautiful corn that you ever saw. Better corn than the Iowa prairie land. Better than any place on earth. I farmed it for years after my father died, but I no longer farm it. I went out of the farming business a good ten years ago. Sold off all the stock and machinery. Now I keep a little kitchen garden. Not too large. It needn't be too large. There is only. . . .'

'You were saying about your brother?'

'Yes, I guess I was. Phil and I were working in the barn one day. It was a rainy day – no, not really a rainy day, just drizzling. We were repairing harness. Yes harness. My father was a strange man in many ways. Strange in reasonable sorts of ways. He didn't believe in using machinery any more than necessary. There was never a tractor on the place. He thought horses were better. On a small place like this, they were. I used them myself until I finally had to sell them. It was an emotional wrench to sell them. The horses and I were friends. But, anyhow, the two of us were working at the harness when Phil said to me, out of the thin air, that he was going to the port and try to get a job on one of the ships. We had talked about it, off and on, before, and both of us had a hankering to go, but it was a surprise to me when Phil spoke up and said that he was going. I had no idea that he had made up his mind. There is something about this that you have to understand – the time, the circumstance, the newness and excitement of travel to the stars in that day of more than fifty years ago. There were days, far back in our history, when New England boys ran off to sea. In that time of fifty years ago, they were running off to space. . . .'

Telling it, he remembered it, as he had told Anderson, as if it were only yesterday. It all came clear and real again, even to the musty scent of last year's hay in the loft above them. Pigeons were cooing in the upper reaches of the barn, and, up in the hillside pasture, a lonesome cow was bawling. The horses stamped in their stalls and made small sounds, munching at the hay remaining in their mangers.

'I made up my mind last night,' said Phil, 'but I didn't tell you because I wanted to be sure. I could wait, of course, but if I wait, there's the chance I'll never go. I don't want to live out my life here wishing I had gone. You'll tell pa, won't you? After I am gone. Sometime this afternoon, giving me a chance to get away.'

'He wouldn't follow you,' said Edward Lambert. 'It would be best for you to tell him. He might reason with you, but he wouldn't stop your going.'

'If I tell him, I will never go,' said Phil. 'I'll see the look upon his face and I'll never go. You'll have to do this much for me, Ed. You'll have to tell him so I won't see the look upon his face.'

'How can you get on a ship? They don't want a green farm boy. They want people who are trained.'

'There'll be a ship,' said Phil, 'that is scheduled to lift off, but with a crew member or two not there. They won't wait for them, they won't waste the time to hunt them down. They'll take anyone who's there. In a day or two, I'll find that kind of ship.'

Lambert remembered once again how he had stood in the barn door, watching his brother walking down the road, his boots splashing in the puddles, his figure blurred by the mist-like drizzle. For a long time after he could no longer see him, long after the grayness of the drizzle had blotted out his form, he had still imagined he could see him, an ever smaller figure trudging down the road. He recalled the tightness in his chest, the choke within his throat, the terrible, gut-twisting heaviness of grief at his brother's leaving. As if a part of him were gone, as if he had been torn in two, as if only half of him were left.

'We were twins,' he told Anderson. 'Identical twins. We were closer than most brothers. We lived in one another's pocket. We did everything together. Each of us felt the same about the other. It took a lot of courage for Phil to walk away like that.'

'And a lot of courage and affection on your part,' said Anderson, 'to let him walk away. But he did come back again?'

'Not for a long time. Not until after both our parents were dead. Then he came walking down the road, just the way he'd left. But he didn't stay. Only for a day or two. He was anxious to be off. As if he were being driven.'

Although that was not exactly right, he told himself. Nervous. Jumpy. Looking back across his shoulder. As if he were being followed. Looking back to make sure the Follower was not there.

'He came a few more times,' he said. 'Years apart. He never stayed too long. He was anxious to get back.'

'How can you explain this idea that people have that you never had a brother?' asked Anderson. 'How do you explain the silence of the records?'

'I have no explanation,' Lambert said. 'People get some strange ideas. A thoughtless rumor starts – perhaps no more than a question: "About this brother of his? Does he really have a brother? Was there ever any brother?" And others pick it up and build it up and it goes on from there. Out in these hills there's not much to talk about. They grab at anything there is. It would be an intriguing thing to talk about – that old fool down in the valley who thinks he has a brother that he never had, bragging about this nonexistent brother out among the stars. Although it seems to me that I never really bragged. I never traded on him.'

'And the records? Or the absence of the records?'

'I just don't know,' said Lambert. 'I didn't know

about the records. I've never checked. There was never any reason to. You see, I know I have a brother.'

'Do you think that you may be getting up to Madison?'

'I know I won't,' said Lambert. 'I seldom leave this place. I no longer have a car. I catch a ride with a neighbor when I can to go to the store and get the few things that I need. I'm satisfied right here. There's no need to go anywhere.'

'You've lived here alone since your parents died?'

'That is right,' said Lambert. 'And I think this has gone far enough. I am not sure I like you, Mr Anderson. Or should that be Dr Anderson? I suspect it should. I'm not going to the university to answer questions that you want me to or to submit to tests in this study of yours. I'm not sure what your interest is and I'm not even faintly interested. I have other, more important things to do.'

Anderson rose from the chair. 'I am sorry,' he said, 'I had not meant. . . .'

'Don't apologize,' said Lambert.

'I wish we could part on a happier note,' said Anderson.

'Don't let it bother you,' said Lambert. 'Just forget about it. That's what I plan to do.'

He continued sitting in the chair long after the visitor had left. A few cars went past, not many, for this was a lightly traveled road, one that really went nowhere, just an access for the few families that lived along the valley and back in the hills.

The gall of the man, he thought, the arrogance of him, to come storming in and asking all those questions. That study of his – perhaps a survey of the fantasies engaged in by an aged population. Although it need not be that; it might be any one of a number of other things.

There was, he cautioned himself, no reason to get upset by it. It was not important; bad manners never were important to anyone but those who practiced them.

He rocked gently back and forth, the rockers complaining on the stones, and gazed across the road and valley to the place along the opposite hill where the creek ran, its waters gurgling over stony shallows and swirling in deep pools. The creek held many memories. There, in long, hot summer days, he and Phil had fished for chubs, using crooked willow branches for rods because there was no money to buy regular fishing gear – not that they would have wanted it even if there had been. In the spring great shoals of suckers had come surging up the creek from the Wisconsin River to reach their spawning areas. He and Phil would go out and seine them, with a seine rigged from a gunny sack, its open end held open by a barrel hoop.

The creek held many memories for him and so did all the land, the towering hills, the little hidden valleys, the heavy hardwood forest that covered all except those few level areas that had been cleared for farming. He knew every path and byway of it. He knew what grew on and lived there and where it grew or lived. He knew of the secrets of the few surrounding square miles of countryside, but not all the secrets; no man was born who could know all the secrets.

He had, he told himself, the best of two worlds. Of two worlds, for he had not told Anderson, he had not told anyone, of that secret link that tied him to Phil. It was a link that never had seemed strange because it was something they had known from the time when they were small. Even apart, they had known what the other might be doing. It was no wondrous thing to them; it was something they had taken very much for granted. Years later, he had read in learned journals the studies that had been made of identical twins with the academic speculation that in some strange manner they seemed to hold telepathic powers which operated only between the two of them – as if they were, in fact, one person in two different bodies.

That was the way of it, most certainly, with him and Phil, although whether it might be telepathy, he had never even wondered until he stumbled on the journals. It did not seem, he thought, rocking in the chair, much like telepathy, for telepathy, as he understood it, was the deliberate sending and receiving of mental messages; it had simply been a knowing of where the other was and what he might be doing. It had been that way when they were youngsters and that way ever since. Not a continued knowing, not continued contact, if it was contact. Through the years, however, it happened fairly often. He had known through all the years since Phil had gone walking down the road the many planets that Phil had visited, the ships he'd traveled on – had seen it all with Phil's eyes, had understood it with Phil's brain, had known the names of the places Phil had seen and understood, as Phil had understood, what had happened in each place. It had not been a conversation: they had not talked with one another; there had been no need to talk. And although Phil had never told him, he was certain Phil had known what he was doing and where he was and what he might be seeing. Even on the few occasions that Phil had come to visit, they had not talked about it; it was no subject for discussion since both accepted it.

In the middle of the afternoon, a beat-up car pulled up before the gate, the motor coughing to a stuttering halt. Jake Hopkins, one of his neighbors up the creek, climbed out, carrying a small basket. He came up on the patio and, setting the basket down, sat down in the other chair.

'Katie sent along a loaf of bread and a blackberry pie,' he said. 'This is about the last of the blackberries. Poor crop this year. The summer was too dry.'

'Didn't do much blackberrying myself this year,' said Lambert. 'Just out a time or two. The best ones are on that ridge over yonder, and I swear that hill gets steeper year by year.'

'It gets steeper for all of us,' said Hopkins. 'You and I, we've been here a long time, Ed.'

'Tell Katie thanks,' said Lambert. 'There ain't no one can make a better pie than she. Pies, I never bother with them, although I purely love them. I do some cooking, of course, but pies takes too much time and fuss.'

'Hear anything about this new critter in the hills?' asked Hopkins.

Lambert chuckled. 'Another one of those wild talks, Jake. Every so often, a couple of times a year, someone starts a story. Remember that one about the swamp beast down at Millville? Papers over in Milwaukee got hold of it, and a sportsman down in Texas read about it and came up with a pack of dogs. He spent three days at Millville, floundering around in the swamps, lost one dog to a rattler, and, so I was told, you never saw a madder white man in your life. He felt that he had been took, and I suppose he was, for there was never any beast. We get bear and panther stories, and there hasn't been a bear or panther in these parts for more than forty years. Once, some years ago some damn fool started a story about a big snake. Big around as a nail keg and thirty feet long. Half the county was out hunting it.'

'Yes, I know,' said Hopkins. 'There's nothing to most of the stories, but Caleb Jones told me one of his boys saw this thing, whatever it may be. Like an ape, or a bear that isn't quite a bear. All over furry, naked. A snowman, Caleb thinks.'

'Well, at least,' said Lambert, 'that is something new. There hasn't been anyone, to my knowledge, claimed to see a snowman here. There have been a lot of reports, however, from the West Coast. It just took a little time to transfer a snowman here.'

'One could have wandered east.'

'I suppose so. If there are any of them out there, that is. I'm not too sure there are.'

'Well, anyhow,' said Hopkins, 'I thought I'd let you know. You are kind of isolated here. No telephone or nothing. You never even run in electricity.'

'I don't need either a telephone or electricity,' said Lambert. 'The only thing about electricity that would tempt me would be a refrigerator. And I don't need that. I got the springhouse over there. It's as good as any refrigerator. Keeps butter sweet for weeks. And a telephone. I don't need a telephone. I have no one to talk to.'

'I'll say this,' said Hopkins. 'You get along all right. Even without a telephone or the electric. Better than most folks.'

'I never wanted much,' said Lambert. 'That's the secret of it – I never wanted much.'

'You working on another book?'

'Jake, I'm always working on another book. Writing down the things I see and hear and the way I feel about them. I'd do it even if no one was interested in them. I'd write it down even if there were no books.'

'You read a lot,' said Hopkins. 'More than most of us.'

'Yes, I guess I do,' said Lambert. 'Reading is a comfort.'

And that was true, he thought. Books lined up on a shelf were a group of friends – not books, but men and women who talked with him across the span of continents and centuries of time. His books, he knew, would not live as some of the others had. They would not long outlast him, but at times he liked to think of the possibility that a hundred years from now someone might find one of his books, in a used book-store, perhaps, and, picking it up, read a few paragraphs of his, maybe liking it well enough to buy it and take it home, where it would rest on the shelves a while, and might, in time, find itself back in a used bookstore again, waiting for someone else to pick it up and read.

It was strange, he thought, that he had written of

things close to home, of those things that most passed by without even seeing, when he could have written of the wonders to be found light-years from earth – the strangenesses that could be found on other planets circling other suns. But of these he had not even thought to write, for they were secret, an inner part of him that was of himself alone, a confidence between himself and Phil that he could not have brought himself to violate.

'We need some rain,' said Hopkins. 'The pastures are going. The pastures on the Jones place are almost bare. You don't see the grass; you see the ground. Caleb has been feeding his cattle hay for the last two weeks, and if we don't get some rain, I'll be doing the same in another week or two. I've got one patch of corn I'll get some nubbins worth the picking, but the rest of it is only good for fodder. It does beat hell. A man can work his tail off some years and come to nothing in the end.'

They talked for another hour or so – the comfortable, easy talk of countrymen who were deeply concerned with the little things that loomed so large for them. Then Hopkins said good-by and, kicking his ramshackle car into reluctant life, drove off down the road.

When the sun was just above the western hills, Lambert went inside and put on a pot of coffee to go with a couple of slices of Katie's bread and a big slice of Katie's pie. Sitting at the table in the kitchen – a table on which he'd eaten so long as memory served – he listened to the ticking of the ancient family clock. The clock, he realized as he listened to it, was symbolic of the house. When the clock talked to him, the house talked to him as well – the house using the clock as a means of communicating with him. Perhaps not talking to him, really, but keeping close in touch, re-minding him that it still was there, that they were together, that they did not stand alone. It had been so through the years; it was more so than ever now, a closer relationship, perhaps arising from the greater need on both their parts.

Although stoutly built by his maternal great-grandfather the house stood in a state of disrepair. There were boards that creaked and buckled when he stepped on them, shingles that leaked in the rainy season. Water streaks ran along the walls, and in the back part of the house, protected by the hill that rose abruptly behind it, where the sun's rays seldom reached, there was the smell of damp and mold.

But the house would last him out, he thought, and that was all that mattered. Once he was no longer here, there'd be no one for it to shelter. It would outlast both him and Phil, but perhaps there would be no need for it to outlast Phil. Out among the stars, Phil had no need of the house. Although, he told himself, Phil would be coming home soon. For he was old and so, he supposed, was Phil. They had, between the two of them, not too many years to wait.

Strange, he thought, that they, who were so much alike, should have lived such different lives – Phil, the wanderer, and he, the stay-at-home, and each of them, despite the differences in their lives, finding so much satisfaction in them.

His meal finished, he went out on the patio again. Behind him, back of the house, the wind soughed through the row of mighty ever-greens, those alien trees planted so many years ago by that old great-grandfather. What a cross-grained conceit, he thought – to plant pines at the base of a hill that was heavy with an ancient growth of oaks and maples, as if to set off the house from the land on which it was erected.

The last of the fireflies were glimmering in the lilac bushes that flanked the gate, and the first of the whippoorwills were crying mournfully up the hollows. Small, wispy clouds partially obscured the skies, but a few stars could be seen. The moon would not rise for another hour or two.

To the north a brilliant star flared out, but watching it, he knew it was not a star. It was a spaceship coming in to land at the port across the river. The flare died out, then flickered on again, and this time did not die out but kept on flaring until the dark line of the horizon cut it off. A moment later, the muted rumble of the landing came to him, and in time it too died out, and he was left alone with the whippoorwills and fireflies.

Someday, on one of those ships, he told himself, Phil would be coming home. He would come striding down the road as he always had before, unannounced but certain of the welcome that would be waiting for him. Coming with the fresh scent of space upon him, crammed with wondrous tales, carrying in his pocket some alien trinket as a gift that, when he was gone, would be placed on the shelf of the old breakfront in the living room, to stand there with the other gifts he had brought on other visits.

There had been a time when he had wished it had been he rather than Phil who had left. God knows, he had ached to go. But once one had gone, there had been no question that the other must stay on. One thing he was proud of – he had never hated Phil for going. They had been too close for hate. There could never be hate between them.

There was something messing around behind him in the pines. For some time now, he had been hearing the rustling but paying no attention to it. It was a coon, most likely, on its way to raid the cornfield that ran along the creek just east of his land. The little animal would find poor pickings there, although there should be enough to satisfy a coon. There seemed to be more rustling than a coon would make. Perhaps it was a family of coons, a mother and her cubs.

Finally, the moon came up, a splendor swimming over the great dark hill behind the house. It was a waning moon that, nevertheless, lightened up the dark. He sat for a while longer and began to feel the chill that every night, even in the summer, came creeping from the creek and flowing up the hollows.

He rubbed an aching knee, then got up slowly and went into the house. He had left a lamp burning on the kitchen table, and now he picked it up, carrying it into the living room and placing it on the table beside an easy chair. He'd read for an hour or so, he told himself, then be off to bed.

As he picked a book off the shelf behind the chair, a knock came at the kitchen door. He hesitated for a moment and the knock came again. Laying down the book, he started for the kitchen, but before he got there, the door opened, and a man came into the kitchen. Lambert stopped and stared at the indistinct blur of the man who'd come into the house. Only a little light came from the lamp in the living room, and he could not be sure.

'Phil?' he asked, uncertain, afraid that he was wrong.

The man stepped forward a pace of two. 'Yes, Ed,' he said. 'You did not recognize me. After all the years, you don't recognize me.'

'It was so dark,' said Lambert, 'that I could not be sure.'

He strode forward with his hand held out, and Phil's hand was there to grasp it. But when their hands met in the handshake, there was nothing there. Lambert's hand close upon itself.

He stood stricken, unable to move, tried to speak and couldn't, the words bubbling and dying and refusing to come out.

'Easy, Ed,' said Phil. 'Take it easy now. That's the way it's always been. Think back. That has to be the way it's always been. I am a shadow only. A shadow of yourself.'

But that could not be right, Lambert told himself. The man who stood there in the kitchen was a solid man, a man of flesh and bone, not a thing of shadow.

'A ghost,' he managed to say. 'You can't be a ghost.'

'Not a ghost,' said Phil. 'An extension of yourself. Surely you had known.'

'No,' said Lambert. 'I did not know. You are my brother, Phil.'

'Let's go into the living room,' said Phil. 'Let's sit down and talk. Let's be reasonable about this. I rather dreaded coming, for I knew you had this thing about a brother. You know as well as I do you never had a brother. You are an only child.'

'But when you were here before. . . .'

'Ed, I've not been here before. If you are only honest with yourself, you'll know I've never been. I couldn't come back, you see, for then you would have known. And up until now, maybe not even now, there was no need for you to know. Maybe I made a mistake in coming back at all.'

'But you talk,' protested Lambert, 'in such a manner as to refute what you are telling me. You speak of yourself as an actual person.'

'And I am, of course,' said Phil. 'You made me such a person. You had to make me a separate person or you couldn't have believed in me. I've been to all the places you have known I've been, done all the things that you know I've done. Not in detail, maybe, but you know the broad outlines of it. Not at first, but later on within a short space of time I became a separate person. I was, in many ways, quite independent of you. Now let's go in and sit down and be comfortable. Let us have this out. Let me make you understand, although in all honesty, you should understand, yourself.'

Lambert turned and stumbled back into the living room and let himself down, fumblingly, into the chair beside the lamp. Phil remained standing, and Lambert, staring at him, saw that Phil was his second self, a man similar to himself, amost identical to himself – the same white hair, the same bushy eyebrows, the same crinkles at the corners of his eyes, the same planes to his face.

He fought for calmness and objectivity. 'A cup of coffee, Phil?' he asked. 'The pot's still on the stove, still warm.'

Phil laughed. 'I cannot drink,' he said, 'or eat. Or a lot of other things. I don't even need to breathe. It's been a trial sometimes, although there have been advantages. They have a name out in the stars for me. A legend. Most people don't believe in me. There are too many legends out there. Some people do believe in me. There are people who'll believe in anything at all.'

'Phil,' said Lambert, 'that day in the barn. When you told me you were leaving, I did stand in the door and watch you walk away.'

'Of course you did,' said Phil. 'You watched me walk away, but you knew then what it was you watched. It was only later that you made me into a brother – a twin brother, was it not?'

'There was a man here from the university,' said Lambert. 'A professor of psychology. He was curious. He had some sort of study going. He'd hunted up the records. He said I never had a brother. I told him he was wrong.'

'You believed what you said,' Phil told him. 'You knew you had a brother. It was a defensive mechanism. You couldn't live with yourself if you had thought otherwise. You couldn't admit the kind of thing you are.'

'Phil, tell me. What kind of thing am I?'

'A breakthrough,' said Phil. 'An evolutionary breakthrough. I've had a lot of time to think about it, and I am sure I'm right. There was no compulsion on my part to hide and obscure the facts, for I was the end result. I hadn't done a thing; you were the one who did it. I had no guilt about it. And I suppose you must have. Otherwise, why all this smokescreen about dear brother Phil.'

'An evolutionary breakthrough, you say. Something like an amphibian becoming a dinosaur?'

'Not that drastic,' said Phil. 'Surely you have heard of people who had several personalities, changing back and forth without warning from one personality to another. But always in the same body. You read the literature on identical twins – one personality in two different bodies. There are stories about people who could mentally travel to distant places, able to report, quite accurately, what they had seen.'

'But this is different, Phil.'

'You still call me Phil.'

'Dammit, you are Phil.'

'Well, then, if you insist. And I am glad you do insist. I'd like to go on being Phil. Different, you say. Of course, it's different. A natural evolutionary progression beyond the other abilities I mentioned. The ability to split your personality and send it out on its own, to make another person that is a shadow of yourself. Not mind alone, something more than mind. Not quite another person, but almost another person. It is an ability that made you different, that set you off from the the rest of the human race. You couldn't face that. No one could. You couldn't admit, not even to yourself, that you were a freak.'

'You've thought a lot about this.'

'Certainly I have. Someone had to. You couldn't, so it was up to me.'

'But I don't remember any of this ability. I still can see you walking off. I have never felt a freak.'

'Certainly not. You built yourself a cover so fast and so secure you even fooled yourself. A man's ability for self-deception is beyond belief.'

Something was scratching at the kitchen door, as a dog might scratch to be let in.

'That's the Follower,' said Phil. 'Go and let him in.'

'But a Follower. . . .'

'That's all right,' said Phil. 'I'll take care of him. The bastard has been following me for years.'

'If it is all right. . . .'

'Sure, it is all right. There's something that he wants, but we can't give it to him.'

Lambert went across the kitchen and opened the door. The Follower came in. Never looking at Lambert, he brushed past him into the living room and skidded to a halt in front of Phil.

'Finally,' shouted the Follower, 'I have run you to your den. Now you cannot elude me. The indignities that you have heaped upon me – the learning of your atrocious language so I could converse with you, the always keeping close behind you, but never catching up, the hilarity of my acquaintances who viewed my obsession with you as an utter madness. But always you fled before me, afraid of me when there was no need of fear. Talk with you, that is all I wanted.'

'I was not afraid of you,' said Phil. 'Why should I have been? You couldn't lay a mitt upon me.'

'Clinging to the outside of a ship when the way was barred inside to get away from me! Riding in the cold and emptiness of space to get away from me. Surviving the cold and space – what kind of creature are you?'

'I only did that once,' said Phil, 'and not to get away from you. I wanted to see what it would be like. I wanted to touch interstellar space, to find out what it was. But I never did find out. And I don't mind telling you that once one got over the wonder and the terror of it, there was very little there. Before the ship touched down, I damn near died of boredom.'

The Follower was a brute, but something about him

said he was more than simple brute. In appearance, he was a cross between a bear and ape, but there was something manlike in him, too. He was a hairy creature, and the clothing that he wore was harness rather than clothing, and the stink of him was enough to make one gag.

'I followed you for years,' he bellowed, 'to ask you a simple question, prepared well to pay you if you give me a useful answer. But you always slip my grasp. If nothing else, you pale and disappear. Why did you do that? Why not wait for me: Why not speak to me? You force me to subterfuge, you force me to set up ambush. In very sneaky and expensive manner, which I deplore, I learned position of your planet and location where you home, so I could come and wait for you to trap you in your den, thinking that even such as you surely must come home again. I prowl the deep woodlands while I wait, and I frighten inhabitants of here, without wishing to, except they blunder on me, and I watch your den and I wait for you, seeing this other of you and thinking he was you, but realizing, upon due observation, he was not. So now. . . .'

'Now just a minute,' said Phil. 'Hold up. There is no reason to explain.'

'But explain you must, for to apprehend you, I am forced to very scurvy trick in which I hold great shame. No open and above board. No honesty. Although one thing I have deduced from my observations. You are no more, I am convinced, than an extension of this other.'

'And now,' said Phil, 'you want to know how it was done. This is the question that you wish to ask.'

'I thank you,' said the Follower, 'for your keen perception, for not forcing me to ask.'

'But first,' said Phil, 'I have a question for you. If we could tell you how it might be done, if we were able to tell you and if you could turn this information to your use, what kind of use would you make of it?'

'Not myself,' said the Follower. 'Not for myself alone,

but for my people, for my race. You see, I never laughed at you; I did not jest about you as so many others did. I did not term you ghost or spook. I knew more to it than that. I saw ability that if rightly used. . . .'

'Now you're getting around to it,' said Phil. 'Now tell us the use.'

'My race,' said the Follower, 'is concerned with many different art forms, working with crude tools and varying skills and in stubborn materials that often take unkindly to the shaping. But I tell myself that if each of us could project ourselves and use our second selves as medium for the art, we could shape as we could wish, creating art forms that are highly plastic, that can be worked over and over again until they attain perfection. And, once perfected, would be immune against time and pilferage. . . .'

'With never a thought,' said Phil, 'as to its use in other ways. In war, in thievery. . . .'

The Follower said, sanctimoniously, 'You cast unworthy aspersions upon my noble race.'

'I am sorry if I do,' said Phil. 'Perhaps it was uncouth of me. And now, as to your question, we simply cannot tell you. Or I don't think that we can tell you. How about it, Ed?'

Lambert shook his head. 'If what both of you say is true, if Phil really is an extension of myself, then I must tell you I do not have the least idea of how it might be done. If I did it, I just did it, that was all. No particular way of doing it. No ritual to perform. No technique I'm aware of.'

'Ridiculous that is,' cried the Follower. 'Surely you can give me hint or clue.'

'All right, then,' said Phil, 'I'll tell you how to do it. Take a species and give them two million years in which they can evolve, and you might come to it. Might, I say. You can't be certain of it. It would have to be the right species, and it must experience the right kind of social and psychological pressure, and it must have the right kind of brain to respond to these kinds of pressures. And if all of this should happen, then one day one member of the species may be able to do what Ed has done. But that one of them is able to do it does not mean that others will. It may be no more than a wild talent, and it may never occur again. So far as we know, it's not happened before. If it has, it's been hidden, as Ed has hidden his ability even from himself, forced to hide it from himself because of the human conditioning that would make such an ability unacceptable.'

'But all these years,' said the Follower, 'all these years, he has kept you as you are. That seems. . . .'

'No,' said Phil. 'Not that at all. No conscious effort on his part. Once he created me, I was self-sustaining.'

'I sense,' the Follower said, sadly, 'that you tell me true. That you hold nothing back.'

'You sense it, hell,' said Phil. 'You read our minds, that is what you did. Why, instead of chasing me across the galaxy, didn't you read my mind long ago and have done with it?'

'You would not stand still,' said the Follower, accusingly. 'You would not talk with me. You never bring this matter to the forefront of your mind so I have a chance to read it.'

'I'm sorry,' said Phil, 'that it turned out this way for you. But until now, you must realize, I could not talk with you. You make the game too good. There was too much zest in it.'

The Follower said, stiffly, 'You look upon me and you think me brute. In your eyes I am. You see no man of honor, no creature of ethics. You know nothing of us and you care even less. Arrogant you are. But, please believe me, in all that's happened, I act with honor according to my light.'

'You must be weary and hungry,' said Lambert. 'Can you eat our food? I could cook up some ham and eggs, and the coffee is still hot. There is a bed for you. It would be an honor to have you as our guest.'

'I thank you for your confidence, for your acceptance of me,' said the Follower. 'It warms – how do you say it – the cockle of the heart. But the mission's done and I must be going now. I have wasted too much time. If you, perhaps, could offer me conveyance to the spaceport.'

'That's something I can't do,' said Lambert. 'You see, I have no car. When I need a ride, I bum one from a neighbor, otherwise I walk.'

'If you can walk, so can I,' said the Follower. 'The spaceport is not far. In a day or two, I'll find a ship that is going out.'

'I wish you'd stay the night,' said Lambert. 'Walking in the dark. . . .'

'Dark is best for me,' said the Follower. 'Less likely to be seen. I gather that few people from other stars wander about this countryside. I have no wish to frighten your good neighbors.'

He turned briskly and went into the kitchen, heading for the door, not waiting for Lambert to open it for him.

'Good-by, pal,' Phil called after him.

The Follower did not answer. He slammed the door behind him.

When Lambert came back into the living room, Phil was standing in front of the fireplace, his elbow on the mantel.

'You know, of course,' he said, 'that we have a problem.'

'Not that I can see,' said Lambert. 'You will stay, won't you. You will not leave again. We are both getting old.'

'If that is what you want. I could disappear, snuff myself out. As if I'd never been. That might be for the best, more comfortable for you. It could be disturbing to have me about. I do not eat or sleep. I can attain a satisfying solidity but only with an effort and only momentarily. I command enough energy to do certain tasks, but not over the long haul.'

'I have had a brother for a long, long time,' said Lambert. 'That's the way I want it. After all this time, I would not want to lose you.'

He glanced at the breakfront and saw that the trinkets Phil had brought on his other trips still stood solidly in place.

Thinking back, he could remember, as if it were only yesterday, watching from the barn door as Phil went trudging down the road through the grey veil of the drizzle.

'Why don't you sit down and tell me,' he said, 'about the incident out in the Coonskin system. I knew about it at the time, of course, but I never caught quite all of it.'

Over the River and Through the Woods

The two children came trudging down the lane in apple-canning time, when the first goldenrods were blooming and the wild asters large in bud. They looked, when she first saw them, out the kitchen window, like children who were coming home from school, for each of them was carrying a bag in which might have been their books. Like Charles and James, she thought, like Alice and Maggie – but the time when those four had trudged the lane on their daily trips to school was in the distant past. Now they had children of their own who made their way to school.

She turned back to the stove to stir the cooking apples, for which the wide-mouthed jars stood waiting on the table, then once more looked out the kitchen window. The two of them were closer now and she could see that the boy was the older of the two – ten, perhaps, and the girl no more than eight.

They might be going past, she thought, although that did not seem too likely, for the lane led to this farm and to nowhere else.

The turned off the lane before they reached the barn and came sturdily trudging up the path that led to the house. There was no hesitation in them; they knew where they were going.

She stepped to the screen door of the kitchen as they came onto the porch and they stopped before the door and stood looking up at her.

The boy said: 'You are our grandma. Papa said we were to say at once that you were our grandma.'

'But that's not . . .,' she said, and stopped. She had been about to say that it was impossible that she was not their grandma. And, looking down into the sober, childish faces, she was glad that she had not said the words.

'I am Ellen,' said the girl, in a piping voice.

'Why, that is strange,' the woman said. 'That is my name, too.'

The boy said, 'My name is Paul.'

She pushed open the door for them and they came in, standing silently in the kitchen, looking all about them as if they'd never seen a kitchen.

'It's just like Papa said,' said Ellen. 'There's the stove and the churn and . . .'

The boy interrupted her. 'Our name is Forbes,' he said.

This time the woman couldn't stop herself. 'Why, that's impossible,' she said. 'That is our name, too.'

The boy nodded solemnly. 'Yes, we knew it was.'

'Perhaps,' the woman said, 'you'd like some milk and cookies.'

'Cookies!' Ellen squealed, delighted.

'We don't want to be any trouble,' said the boy. 'Papa said we were to be no trouble.'

'He said we should be good,' piped Ellen.

'I am sure you will be,' said the woman, 'and you are no trouble.'

In a little while, she thought, she'd get it straightened out.

She went to the stove and set the kettle with the cooking apples to one side, where they would simmer slowly.

'Sit down at the table,' she said. 'I'll get the milk and cookies.'

She glanced at the clock, ticking on the shelf. Four o'clock, almost. In just a little while the men would come in from the fields. Jackson Forbes would know what to do about this; he had always known.

They climbed up on two chairs and sat there solemnly, staring all about them, at the ticking clock, at the wood stove with the fire glow showing through its draft, at the wood piled in the wood box, at the butter churn standing in the corner.

They set their bags on the floor beside them, and they were strange bags, she noticed. They were made of heavy cloth or canvas, but there were no drawstrings or no straps to fasten them. But they were closed, she saw, despite no straps or strings.

'Do you have some stamps?' asked Ellen.

'Stamps?' asked Mrs Forbes.

'You must pay no attention to her,' said Paul. 'She should not have asked you. She asks everyone and Mama told her not to.'

'But stamps?'

'She collects them. She goes around snitching letters that other people have. For the stamps on them, you know.'

'Well now,' said Mrs Forbes, 'there may be some old letters. We'll look for them later on.'

She went into the pantry and got the earthen jug of milk and filled a plate with cookies from the jar. When she came back they were sitting there sedately, waiting for the cookies.

'We are here just for a little while,' said Paul. 'Just a short vacation. Then our folks will come and get us and take us back again.'

Ellen nodded her head vigorously. 'That's what they told us when we went. When I was afraid to go.'

'You were afraid to go?'

'Yes. It was all so strange.'

'There was so little time,' said Paul. 'Almost none at all. We had to leave so fast.'

'And where are you from?' asked Mrs Forbes.

'Why,' said the boy, 'just a little ways from here. We walked just a little ways and of course we had the map. Papa gave it to us and he went over it carefully with us. . . .'

'You're sure your name is Forbes?'

Ellen bobbed her head. 'Of course it is,' she said.

'Strange,' said Mrs Forbes. And it was more than strange, for there were no other Forbes in the neighborhood except her children and her grandchildren and these two, no matter what they said, were strangers.

They were busy with the milk and cookies and she went back to the stove and set the kettle with the apples back on the front again, stirring the cooking fruit with a wooden spoon.

'Where is Grandpa?' Ellen asked.

'Grandpa's in the field. He'll be coming in soon. Are you finished with your cookies?'

'All finished,' said the girl.

'Then we'll have to set the table and get the supper cooking. Perhaps you'd like to help me.'

Ellen hopped down off the chair. 'I'll help,' she said.

'And I,' said Paul, 'will carry in some wood. Papa said I should be helpful. He said I could carry in the wood and feed the chickens and hunt the eggs and . . .'

'Paul,' said Mrs Forbes, 'it might help if you'd tell me what your father does.'

'Papa,' said the boy, 'is a temporal engineer.'

The two hired men sat at the kitchen table with the checker board between them. The two older people were in the living room.

'You never saw the likes of it,' said Mrs Forbes. 'There was this piece of metal and you pulled it and it ran along another metal strip and the bag came open. And you pulled it the other way and the bag was closed.'

'Something new,' said Jackson Forbes. 'There may be many new things we haven't heard about, back here in the sticks. There are inventors turning out all sorts of things.'

'And the boy,' she said, 'has the same thing on his trousers. I picked them up from where he threw them on the floor when he went to bed and I folded them and put them on the chair. And I saw this strip of metal, the edges jagged-like. And the clothes they wear. That boy's trousers are cut off above the knees and the dress that the girl was wearing was so short. . . .'

'They talked of plains,' mused Jackson Forbes, 'but not the plains we know. Something that is used, apparently, for folks to travel in. And rockets – as if there were rockets every day and not just on the Earth.'

'We couldn't question them, of course,' said Mrs Forbes. 'There was something about them, something that I sensed.'

Her husband nodded. 'They were frightened, too.'

'You are frightened, Jackson?'

'I don't know,' he said, 'but there are no other Forbes. Not close, that is. Charlie is the closest and he's five miles away. And they said they walked just a little piece.'

'What are you going to do?' she asked. 'What can we do?'

'I don't rightly know,' he said. 'Drive in to the county seat and talk with the sheriff, maybe. These children must be lost. There must be someone looking for them.'

'But they don't act as if they're lost,' she told him. 'They knew they were coming here. They knew we would be here. They told me I was their grandma and they asked after you and they called you Grandpa. And they are so sure. They don't act as if we're strangers. They've been told about us. They said they'd stay just a little while and that's the way they act. As if they'd just come for a visit.'

'I think,' said Jackson Forbes, 'that I'll hitch up Nellie after breakfast and drive around the neighborhood and ask some questions. Maybe there'll be someone who can tell me something.'

'The boy said his father was a temporal engineer. That just don't make sense. Temporal means the worldly power and authority and . . .'

'It might be some joke,' her husband said. 'Something that the father said in jest and the son picked up as truth.'

'I think,' said Mrs Forbes, 'I'll go upstairs and see if they're asleep. I left their lamps turned low. They are so little and the house is strange to them. If they are asleep, I'll blow out the lamps.'

Jackson Forbes grunted his approval. 'Dangerous,' he said, 'to keep lights burning of the night. Too much chance of fire.'

The boy was asleep, flat upon his back – the deep and healthy sleep of youngsters. He had thrown his clothes upon the floor when he had undressed to go to bed, but now they were folded neatly on the chair, where she had placed them when she had gone into the room to say goodnight.

The bag stood beside the chair and it was open, the two rows of jagged metal gleaming dully in the dim glow of the lamp. Within its shadowed interior lay the dark forms of jumbled possessions, disorderly, and helter-skelter, no way for a bag to be.

She stooped and picked up the bag and set it on the chair and reached for the little metal tab to close it. At least, she told herself, it should be closed and not left standing open. She grasped the tab and it slid smoothly along the metal tracks and then stopped, its course obstructed by an object that stuck out.

She saw it was a book and reached down to rearrange it so she could close the bag. And as she did so, she saw the title in its faint gold lettering across the leather backstrap – Holy Bible.

With her fingers grasping the book, she hesitated for a moment, then slowly drew it out. It was bound in an expensive black leather that was dulled with age. The edges were cracked and split and the leather worn from long usage. The gold edging of the leaves were faded.

Hesitantly, she opened it and there, upon the fly leaf, in old and faded ink, was the inscription:

> *To Sister Ellen*
> *from Amelia*
> *Oct. 30, 1896*
> *Many Happy Returns of the Day*

She felt her knees grow weak and she let herself carefully to the floor and there, crouched beside the chair, read the fly leaf once again.

30 October 1896 – that was her birthday, certainly, but it had not come as yet, for this was only the beginning of September, 1896.

And the Bible – how old was this Bible she held within her hands? A hundred years, perhaps, more than a hundred years.

A Bible, she thought – exactly the kind of gift Amelia would give her. But a gift that had not been given yet, one that could not be given, for that day upon the fly leaf was a month into the future.

It couldn't be, of course. It was some kind of stupid joke. Or some mistake. Or a coincidence, perhaps. Somewhere else someone else was named Ellen and also had a sister who was named Amelia and the date was a mistake – someone had written the wrong year. It would be an easy thing to do.

But she was not convinced. They had said the name

was Forbes and they had come straight here and Paul
had spoken of a map so they could find the way.

Perhaps there were other things inside the bag. She
looked at it and shook her head. She shouldn't pry. It
had been wrong to take the Bible out.

On 30 October she would be fifty-nine – an old
farm-wife with married sons and daughters and
grandchildren who came to visit her on week-end and on
holidays. And a sister Amelia who, in this year of 1896,
would give her a Bible as a birthday gift.

Her hands shook as she lifted the Bible and put it back
into the bag. She'd talk to Jackson when she went down
stairs. He might have some thought upon the matter and
he'd know what to do.

She tucked the book back into the bag and pulled the
tab and the bag was closed. She set it on the floor again
and looked at the boy upon the bed. He still was fast
asleep, so she blew out the light.

In the adjoining room little Ellen slept, baby-like,
upon her stomach. The low flame of the turned-down
lamp flickered gustily in the breeze that came through an
open window.

Ellen's bag was closed and stood squared against the
chair with a sense of neatness. The woman looked at it
and hesitated for a moment, then moved on around the
bed to where the lamp stood on a bedside table.

The children were asleep and everything was well and
she'd blow out the light and go downstairs and talk with
Jackson, and perhaps there'd be no need for him to hitch
up Nellie in the morning and drive around to ask
questions of the neighbors.

As she leaned to blow out the lamp, she saw the
envelope upon the table, with the two large stamps of
many colors affixed to the upper right-hand corner.

Such pretty stamps, she thought – I never saw so

pretty. She leaned closer to take a look at them and saw the country name upon them. Israel. But there was no such actual place as Israel. It was a Bible name, but there was no country. And if there were no country, how could there be stamps?

She picked up the envelope and studied the stamp, making sure that she had seen right. Such a pretty stamp!

She collects them, Paul had said. She's always snitching letters that belong to other people.

The envelope bore a postmark, and presumably a date, but it was blurred and distorted by a hasty, sloppy cancellation and she could not make it out.

The edge of a letter sheet stuck a quarter inch out of the ragged edges where the envelope had been torn open and she pulled it out, gasping in her haste to see it while an icy fist of fear was clutching at her heart.

It was, she saw, only the end of a letter, the last page of a letter, and it was in type rather than in longhand – type like one saw in a newspaper or a book.

Maybe one of those new-fangled things they had in big city offices, she thought, the ones she'd read about. Typewriters – was that what they were called?

do not believe, the one page read, *your plan is feasible. There is no time. The aliens are closing in and they will not give us time.*

And there is the further consideration of the ethics of it, even if it could be done. We can not, in all conscience, scurry back into the past and visit our problems upon the people of a century ago. Think of the problems it would create for them, the economic confusion and the psychological effect.

If you feel that you must, at least, send the children back, think a moment of the wrench it will give those two good souls when they realize the truth. Theirs is a smug and solid world – sure and safe and sound. The concepts of this mad century would destroy all they have, all that they believe in.

But I suppose I cannot presume to counsel you. I have done what you asked. I have written you all I know of our old ancestors back on that Wisconsin farm. As historian of the family, I am sure my facts are right. Use them as you see fit and God have mercy on us all.

Your loving brother,
Jackson

P.S. A suggestion. If you do send the children back, you might send along with them a generous supply of the new cancer-inhibitor drug. Great-great-grandmother Forbes died in 1904 of a condition that I suspect was cancer. Given those pills, she might survive another ten or twenty years. And what, I ask you, brother, would that mean to this tangled future? I don't pretend to know. It might save us. It might kill us quicker. It might have no effect at all. I leave the puzzle to you.

If I can finish up work here and get away, I'll be with you at the end.

Mechanically she slid the letter back into the envelope and laid it upon the table beside the flaring lamp.

Slowly she moved to the window that looked out on the empty lane.

They will come and get us, Paul had said. But would they ever come. Could they ever come?

She found herself wishing they would come. Those poor people, those poor frightened children caught so far in time.

Blood of my blood, she thought, flesh of my flesh, so many years away. But still her flesh and blood, no matter how removed. Not only these two beneath this roof tonight, but all those others who had not come to her.

The letter had said 1904 and cancer and that was eight years away – she'd be an old, old woman then. And the signature had been Jackson – an old family name, she wondered, carried on and on, a long chain of people who bore the name of Jackson Forbes?

She was stiff and numb, she knew. Later she'd be

frightened. Later she would wish she had not read the letter. Perhaps, she did not know.

But now she must go back downstairs and tell Jackson the best way that she could.

She moved across the room and blew out the light and went out into the hallway.

A voice came from the open door beyond.

'Grandma, is that you?'

'Yes, Paul,' she answered. 'What can I do for you?'

In the doorway she saw him crouched beside the chair, in the shaft of moonlight pouring through the window, fumbling at the bag.

'I forgot,' he said. 'There was something papa said I was to give you right away.'

Auk House

David Latimer was lost when he found the house. He had set out for Wyalusing, a town he had only heard of but had never visited, and apparently had taken the wrong road. He had passed through two small villages, Excelsior and Navarre, and if the roadside signs were right, in another few miles he would be coming into Montfort. He hoped that someone in Montfort could set him right again.

The road was a county highway, crooked and narrow and bearing little traffic. It twisted through the rugged headlands that ran down to the coast, flanked by birch and evergreens and rarely out of reach of the muted thunder of surf pounding on giant boulders that lay tumbled on the shore.

The car was climbing a long, steep hill when he first saw the house, between the coast and road. It was a sprawling pile of brick and stone, flaunting massive twin chimneys at either end of it, sited in front of a grove of ancient birch and set so high upon the land that it seemed to float against the sky. He slowed the car, pulled over to the roadside, and stopped to have a better look at it.

A semicircular brick-paved driveway curved up to the entrance of the house. A few huge oak trees grew on the well-kept lawn, and in their shade stood graceful stone benches that had the look of never being used.

There was, it seemed to Latimer, a pleasantly haunted look to the place – a sense of privacy, of olden dignity, a withdrawal from the world. On the front lawn, marring it, desecrating it, stood a large planted sign:

FOR RENT OR SALE
See Campbell's Realty – Half Mile Down the Road

And an arrow pointing to show which way down the road.

Latimer made no move to continue down the road. He sat quietly in the car, looking at the house. The sea, he thought, was just beyond; from a second-story window at the back, one could probably see it.

It had been word of a similar retreat that had sent him seeking out Wyalusing – a place where he could spend a quiet few months at painting. A more modest place, perhaps, than this, although the description he had been given of it had been rather sketchy.

Too expensive, he thought, looking at the house; most likely more than he could afford, although with the last couple of sales he had made, he was momentarily flush. However, it might not be as expensive as he thought, he told himself; a place like this would have small attraction for most people. Too big, but for himself that would make no difference; he could camp out in a couple of rooms for the few months he would be there.

Strange, he reflected, the built-in attraction the house had for him, the instinctive, spontaneous attraction, the instant knowing that this was the sort of place he had had in mind. Not knowing until now that it was the sort of place he had in mind. Old, he told himself – a century, two centuries, more than likely. Built by some now forgotten lumber baron. Not lived in, perhaps, for a number of years. There would be bats and mice.

He put the car in gear and moved slowly out into the road, glancing back over his shoulder at the house. A half mile down the road, at the edge of what probably was Montfort, although there was no sign to say it was, on the right-hand side, a lopsided, sagging sign on an old, lopsided shack, announced Campbell's Realty. Hardly intending to do it, his mind not made up as yet, he pulled the car off the road and parked in front of the shack.

Inside, a middle-aged man dressed in slacks and turtleneck sat with his feet propped on a littered desk.

'I dropped in,' said Latimer, 'to inquire about the house down the road. The one with the brick drive.'

'Oh, that one,' said the man. 'Well, I tell you, stranger, I can't show it to you now. I'm waiting for someone who wants to look at the Ferguson place. Tell you what, though. I could give you the key.'

'Could you give me some idea of what the rent would be?'

'Why don't you look at it first. See what you think of it. Get the feel of it. See if you'd fit into it. If you like it, we can talk. Hard place to move. Doesn't fit the needs of many people. Too big, for one thing, too old. I could get you a deal on it.'

The man took his feet off the desk, plopped them on the floor. Rummaging in a desk drawer, he came up with a key with a tag attached to it and threw it on the desk top.

'Have a look at it and then come back,' he said. 'This Ferguson business shouldn't take more than an hour or two.'

'Thank you,' said Latimer, picking up the key.

He parked the car in front of the house and went up the steps. The key worked easily in the lock and the door swung open on well-oiled hinges. He came into a hall that ran from front to back, with a staircase ascending to the second floor and doors opening on either side into ground-floor rooms.

The hall was dim and cool, a place of graciousness.

When he moved along the hall, the floorboards did not creak beneath his feet as in a house this old he would have thought they might. There was no shut-up odor, no smell of damp or mildew, no sign of bats or mice.

The door to his right was open, as were all the doors that ran along the hall. He glanced into the room – a large room, with light from the westering sun flooding through the windows that stood on either side of a marble fireplace. Across the hall was a smaller room, with a fireplace in one corner. A library or a study, he thought. The larger room, undoubtedly, had been thought of, when the house was built, as a drawing room. Beyond the larger room, on the right-hand side, he found what might have been a kitchen with a large brick fireplace that had a utilitarian look to it – used, perhaps, in the olden days for cooking, and across from it a much larger room, with another marble fireplace, windows on either side of it and oblong mirrors set into the wall, an ornate chandelier hanging from the ceiling. This, he knew, had to be the dining room, the proper setting for leisurely formal dinners.

He shook his head at what he saw. It was much too grand for him, much larger, much more elegant than he had thought. If someone wanted to live as a place like this should be lived in, it would cost a fortune in furniture alone. He had told himself that during a summer's residence he could camp out in a couple of rooms, but to camp out in a place like this would be sacrilege; the house deserved a better occupant than that.

Yet, it still held its attraction. There was about it a sense of openness, of airiness, of ease. Here a man would not be cramped; he'd have room to move about. It conveyed a feeling of well-being. It was, in essence, not a living place, but a place for living.

The man had said that it had been hard to move, that

to most people it had slight appeal – too large, too old – and that he could make an attractive deal on it. But, with a sinking feeling, Latimer knew that what the man had said was true. Despite its attractiveness, it was far too large. It would take too much furniture even for a summer of camping out. And yet, despite all this, the pull – almost a physical pull – toward it still hung on.

He went out the back door of the hall, emerging on a wide veranda that ran the full length of the house. Below him lay the slope of ancient birch, running down a smooth green lawn to the seashore studded by tumbled boulders that flung up white clouds of spume as the racing waves broke against them. Flocks of mewling birds hung above the surging surf like white phantoms, and beyond this, the gray-blue stretch of ocean ran to the far horizon.

This was the place, he knew, that he had hunted for – a place of freedom that would free his brush from the conventions that any painter, at times, felt crowding in upon him. Here lay that remoteness from all other things, a barrier set up against a crowding world. Not objects to paint, but a place in which to put upon his canvases that desperate crying for expression he felt within himself.

He walked down across the long stretch of lawn, among the age-striped birch, and came upon the shore. He found a boulder and sat upon it, feeling the wild exhilaration of wind and water, sky and loneliness.

The sun had set and quiet shadows crept across the land. It was time to go, he told himself, but he kept on sitting, fascinated by the delicate deepening of the dusk, the subtle color changes that came upon the water.

When he finally roused himself and started walking up the lawn, the great birch trees had assumed a ghostliness that glimmered in the twilight. He did not go back into the house, but walked around it to come out on the front.

He reached the brick driveway and started walking, remembering that he'd have to go back into the house to lock the back door off the hall.

It was not until he had almost reached the front entrance that he realized his car was gone. Confused, he stopped dead in his tracks. He had parked it there; he was sure he had. Was it possible he had parked it off the road and walked up the drive, now forgetting that he had?

He turned and started down the driveway, his shoes clicking on the bricks. No, dammit, he told himself, I did drive up the driveway – I remember doing it. He looked back and there wasn't any car, either in front of the house or along the curve of driveway. He broke into a run, racing down the driveway toward the road. Some kids had come along and pushed it to the road – that must be the answer. A juvenile prank, the pranksters hiding somewhere, tittering to themselves as they watched him run to find it. Although that was wrong, he thought – he had left it set on 'Park' and locked. Unless they broke a window, there was no way they could have pushed it.

The brick driveway came to an end and there wasn't any road. The lawn and driveway came down to where they ended, and at that point a forest rose up to block the way. A wild and tangled forest that was very dark and dense, great trees standing up where the road had been. To his nostrils came the damp scent of forest mold, and somewhere in the darkness of the trees, an owl began to hoot.

He swung around, to face back toward the house, and saw the lighted windows. It couldn't be, he told himself quite reasonably. There was no one in the house, no one to turn on the lights. In all likelihood, the electricity was shut off.

But the lighted windows persisted. There could be no

question there were lights. Behind him, he could hear the strange rustlings of the trees and now there were two owls, answering one another.

Reluctantly, unbelievingly, he started up the driveway. There must be some sort of explanation. Perhaps, once he had the explanation, it would all seem quite simple. He might have gotten turned around somehow, as he had somehow gotten turned around earlier in the day, taking the wrong road. He might have suffered a lapse of memory, for some unknown and frightening reason have experienced a blackout. This might not be the house he had gone to look at, although, he insisted to himself, it certainly looked the same.

He came up the brick driveway and mounted the steps that ran up to the door, and while he was still on the steps, the door came open and a man in livery stepped aside to let him in.

'You are a little late, sir,' said the man. 'We had expected you some time ago. The others waited for you, but just now went in to dinner, thinking you had been unavoidably detained. Your place is waiting for you.'

Latimer hesitated.

'It is quite all right, sir,' said the man. 'Except on special occasions, we do not dress for dinner. You're all right as you are.'

The hall was lit by short candles set in sconces on the wall. Paintings also hung there, and small sofas and a few chairs were lined along the wall. From the dining room came the sound of conversation.

The butler closed the door and started down the hall. 'If you would follow me, sir.'

It was all insane, of course. It could not be happening. It was something he imagined. He was standing out there, on the bricks of the driveway, with the forest and the hooting owls behind him, imagining that he was here, in this dimly lighted hallway with the talk and laughter coming from the dining room.

'Sir,' said the butler, 'if you please.'

'But, I don't understand. This place, an hour ago . . .'

'The others are all waiting for you. They have been looking forward to you. You must not keep them waiting.'

'All right, then,' said Latimer. 'I shall not keep them waiting.'

At the entrance to the dining room, the butler stood aside so that he could enter.

The others were seated at a long, elegantly appointed table. The chandelier blazed with burning tapers. Uniformed serving maids stood against one wall. A sideboard gleamed with china and cut glass. There were bouquets of flowers upon the table.

A man dressed in a green sports shirt and a corduroy jacket rose from the table and motioned to him.

'Latimer, over here,' he said. 'You are Latimer, are you not?'

'Yes, I'm Latimer.'

'Your place is over here, between Enid and myself. We'll not bother with introductions now. We can do that later on.'

Scarcely feeling his feet making contact with the floor, moving in a mental haze, Latimer went down the table. The man who stood had remained standing, thrusting out a beefy hand. Latimer took it and the other's handshake was warm and solid.

'I'm Underwood,' he said. 'Here, sit down. Don't stand on formality. We've just started on the soup. If yours is cold, we can have another brought to you.'

'Thank you,' said Latimer. 'I'm sure it's all right.'

On the other side of him, Enid said, 'We waited for you. We knew that you were coming, but you took so long.'

'Some,' said Underwood, 'take longer than others. It's just the way it goes.'

'But I don't understand,' said Latimer. 'I don't know what's going on.'

'You will,' said Underwood. 'There's really nothing to it.'

'Eat your soup,' Enid urged. 'It is really good. We get such splendid chowder here.'

She was small and dark of hair and eyes, a strange intensity in her.

Latimer lifted the spoon and dipped it in the soup. Enid was right; it was a splendid chowder.

The man across the table said, 'I'm Charlie. We'll talk later on. We'll answer any questions.'

The woman sitting beside Charlie said, 'You see, we don't understand it, either. But it's all right. I'm Alice.'

The maids were removing some of the soup bowls and bringing on the salads. On the sideboard the china and cut glass sparkled in the candlelight. The flowers on the table were peonies. There were, with himself, eight people seated at the table.

'You see,' said Latimer, 'I only came to look at the house.'

'That's the way,' said Underwood, 'that it happened to the rest of us. Not just recently. Years apart. Although I don't know how many years. Jonathon, down there at the table's end, that old fellow with a beard, was the first of us. The others straggled in.'

'The house,' said Enid, 'is a trap, very neatly baited. We are mice caught in a trap.'

From across the table, Alice said, 'She makes it sound so dreadful. It's not that way at all. We are taken care of meticulously. There is a staff that cooks our food and serves it, that makes our beds, that keeps all clean and neat . . .'

'But who would want to trap us?'

'That,' said Underwood, 'is the question we all try to solve – except for one or two of us, who have become resigned. But, although there are several theories, there is no solution. I sometimes ask myself what difference it makes. Would we feel any better if we knew our trappers?'

A trap neatly baited, Latimer thought, and indeed it had been. There had been that instantaneous, instinctive attraction that the house had held for him – even only driving past it, the attraction had reached out for him.

The salad was excellent, and so were the steak and baked potato. The rice pudding was the best Latimer had ever eaten. In spite of himself, he found that he was enjoying the meal, the bright and witty chatter that flowed all around the table.

In the drawing room, once dinner was done, they sat in front of a fire in the great marble fireplace.

'Even in the summer,' said Enid, 'when night come on, it gets chilly here. I'm glad it does, because I love a fire. We have a fire almost every night.'

'We?' said Latimer. 'You speak as if you were a tribe.'

'A band,' she said. 'A gang, perhaps. Fellow conspirators, although there's no conspiracy. We get along together. That's one thing that is so nice about it. We get along so well.'

The man with the beard came over to Latimer. 'My name is Jonathon,' he said. 'We were too far apart at dinner to become acquainted.'

'I am told,' said Latimer, 'that you are the one who has been here the longest.'

'I am now,' said Jonathon. 'Up until a couple of years ago, it was Peter. Old Pete, we used to call him.'

'Used to?'

'He died,' said Enid. 'That's how come there was room for you. There is only so much room in this house, you see.'

'You mean it took two years to find someone to replace him.'

'I have a feeling,' said Jonathon, 'that we belong to a select company. I would think that you might have to possess rather rigid qualifications before you were considered.'

'That's what puzzles me,' said Latimer. 'There must be some common factor in the group. The kind of work we're in, perhaps.'

'I am sure of it,' said Jonathon. 'You are a painter, are you not?'

Latimer nodded. 'Enid is a poet,' said Jonathon, 'and a very good one. I aspire to philosophy, although I'm not too good at it. Dorothy is a novelist and Alice a musician – a pianist. Not only does she play, but she can compose as well. You haven't met Dorothy or Jane as yet.'

'No. I think I know who they are, but I haven't met them.'

'You will,' said Enid, 'before the evening's over. Our group is so small we get to know one another well.'

'Could I get a drink for you?' asked Jonathon.

'I would appreciate it. Could it be Scotch, by any chance?'

'It could be,' said Jonathon, 'anything you want. Ice or water?'

'Ice, if you would. But I feel I am imposing.'

'No one imposes here,' said Jonathon. 'We take care of one another.'

'And if you don't mind,' said Enid, 'one for me as well. You know what I want.'

As Jonathon walked away to get the drinks, Latimer said to Enid, 'I must say that you've all been kind to me. You took me in, a stranger . . .'

'Oh, not a stranger really. You'll never be a stranger. Don't you understand? You are one of us. There was an empty place and you've filled it. And you'll be here forever. You'll never go away.'

'You mean that no one ever leaves?'

'We try. All of us have tried. More than once for some of us. But we've never made it. Where is there to go?'

'Surely there must be someplace else. Some way to get back.'

'You don't understand,' she said. 'There is no place but here. All the rest is wilderness. You could get lost if you weren't careful. There have been times when we've had to go out and hunt down the lost ones.'

Underwood came across the room and sat down on the sofa on the other side of Enid.

'How are you two getting on?' he said.

'Very well,' said Enid. 'I was just telling David there's no way to get away from here.'

'That is fine,' said Underwood, 'but it will make no difference. There'll come a day he'll try.'

'I suppose he will,' said Enid, 'but if he understands beforehand, it will be easier.'

'The thing that rankles me,' said Latimer, 'is why. You said at the dinner table everyone tries for a solution, but no one ever finds one.'

'Not exactly that,' said Underwood. 'I said there are some theories. But the point is that there is no way for us to know which one of them is right. We may have already guessed the reason for it all, but the chances are we'll never know. Enid has the most romantic notion. She thinks we are being held by some super-race from some far point in the galaxy who want to study us. We are specimens, you understand. They cage us in what amounts to a laboratory, but do not intrude upon us. They want to observe us under natural conditions and see what makes us tick. And under these conditions, she thinks we should act as civilized as we can manage.'

'I don't know if I really think that,' said Enid, 'but it's

a nice idea. It's no crazier than some of the other explanations. Some of us have theorized that we are being given a chance to do the best work we can. Someone is taking all economic pressure off us, placing us in a pleasant environment, and giving us all the time we need to develop whatever talents we may have. We're being subsidized.'

'But what good would that do?' asked Latimer. 'I gather we are out of touch with the world we knew. No matter what we did, who is there to know?'

'Not necessarily,' said Underwood. 'Things disappear. One of Alice's compositions and one of Dorothy's novels and a few of Enid's poems.'

'You think someone is reaching in and taking them? Being quite selective?'

'It's just a thought,' said Underwood. 'Some of the things we create do disappear. We hunt for them and we never find them.'

Jonathon came back with the drinks. 'We'll have to settle down now,' he said, 'and quite all this chatter. Alice is about to play. Chopin, I believe she said.'

It was late when Latimer was shown to his room by Underwood, up on the third floor. 'We shifted around a bit to give this one to you,' said Underwood. 'It's the only one that has a skylight. You haven't got a straight ceiling – it's broken by the roofline – but I think you'll find it comfortable.'

'You knew that I was coming, then, apparently some time before I arrived.'

'Oh, yes, several days ago. Rumors from the staff; the staff seems to know everything. But not until late yesterday did we definitely know when you would arrive.'

After Underwood said good night, Latimer stood for a time in the center of the room. There was a skylight, as Underwood had said, positioned to supply a north light.

Standing underneath it was an easel, and stacked against the wall were blank canvases. There would be paint and brushes, he knew, and everything else that he might need. Whoever or whatever had sucked him into this place would do everything up brown; nothing would be overlooked.

It was unthinkable, he told himself, that it could have happened. Standing now, in the center of the room, he still could not believe it. He tried to work out the sequence of events that had led him to this house, the steps by which he had been lured into the trap, if trap it was – and on the face of the evidence, it had to be a trap. There had been the realtor in Boston who had told him of the house in Wyalusing. 'It's the kind of place you are looking for,' he had said. 'No near neighbors, isolated. The little village a couple of miles down the road. If you need a woman to come in a couple of times a week to keep the place in order, just ask in the village. There's bound to be someone you could hire. The place is surrounded by old fields that haven't been farmed in years and are going back to brush and thickets. The coast is only half a mile distant. If you like to do some shooting, come fall there'll be quail and grouse. Fishing, too, if you want to do it.'

'I might drive up and have a look at it,' he had told the agent, who had then proceeded to give him the wrong directions, putting him on the road that would take him past this place. Or had he? Had he, perhaps, been his own muddleheadedness that had put him on the wrong road? Thinking about it, Latimer could not be absolutely certain. The agent had given him directions, but had they been the wrong directions? In the present situation, he knew that he had the tendency to view all prior circumstances with suspicion. Yet, certainly, there had been some psychological pressure brought, some mis-direction employed to bring him to this house. It could not have been simple happenstance that had brought him here, to a house that trapped practitioners of the arts. A poet, a musician, a novelist, and a philosopher – although, come to think of it, a philosopher did not seem to exactly fit the pattern. Maybe the pattern was more apparent, he told himself, than it actually was. He still did not know the professions of Underwood, Charlie, and Jane. Maybe, once he did know, the pattern would be broken.

A bed stood in one corner of the room, a bedside table and a lamp beside it. In another corner three comfortable chairs were grouped, and along a short section of the wall stood shelves that were filled with books. On the wall beside the shelves hung a painting. It was only after staring at it for several minutes that he recognized it. It was one of his own, done several years ago.

He moved across the carpeted floor to confront the painting. It was one of those to which he had taken a special liking – one that, in fact, he had been somewhat reluctant to let go, would not have sold it if he had not stood so much in need of money.

The subject sat on the back stoop of a tumbledown house. Beside him, where he had dropped it, was a newspaper folded to the 'Help Wanted' ads. From the breast pocket of his painfully clean, but worn, work shirt an envelope stuck out, the gray envelope in which welfare checks were issued. The man's work-scarred hands, lay listlessly in his lap, the forearms resting on the thighs, which were clad in ragged denims. He had not shaved for several days and the graying whiskers lent a deathly gray cast to his face. His hair, in need of barbering, was a tangled rat's nest, and his eyes, deep-set beneath heavy, scraggly brows, held a sense of helplessness. A scrawny cat sat at one corner of the house, a broken bicycle leaned against the basement wall. The man was looking out over a backyard filled with various kinds of litter, and beyond it the open countryside, a dingy gray and brown, seared by drought and lack of care, while on the horizon was the hint of industrial chimneys, gaunt and stark, with faint wisps of smoke trailing from them.

The painting was framed in heavy gilt – not the best choice, he thought, for such a piece. The bronze title tag was there, but he did not bend to look at it. He knew what it would say:

UNEMPLOYED
David Lloyd Latimer

How long ago? he wondered. Five years, or was it six? A man by the name of Johnny Brown, he remembered, had been the model. Johnny was a good man and he had used him several times. Later on, when he had tried to find him, he had been unable to locate him. He had not been seen for months in his old haunts along the waterfront and no one seemed to know where he had gone.

Five years ago, six years ago – sold to put bread into his belly, although that was silly, for when did he ever paint other than for bread? And here it was. He tried to recall the purchaser, but was unable to.

There was a closet, and when he opened it, he found a row of brand-new clothes, boots and shoes lined up on the floor, hats ranged neatly on the shelf. And all of them would fit – he was sure they would. The setters and the baiters of this trap would have seen to that. In the highboy next to the bed would be underwear, shirts, sock, sweaters – the kind that he would buy.

'We are taken care of,' Enid had told him, sitting on the sofa with him before the flaring fire. There could be, he told himself, no doubt of that. No harm was intended them. They, in fact, were coddled.

And the question: Why? Why a few hand-picked people selected from many millions?

He walked to a window and stood looking out of it.
The room was in the back of the house so that he looked
down across the grove of ghostly birch. The moon had
risen and hung like a milk-glass globe above the dark
blur of the ocean. High as he stood, he could see the
whiteness of the spray breaking on the boulders.

He had to have time to think, he told himself, time to
sort it out, to get straight in his mind all the things that
had happened in the last few hours. There was no sense
in going to bed; tense as he was, he'd never get to sleep.
He could not think in this room, nor, perhaps, in the
house. He had to go some place that was uncluttered.
Perhaps if he went outside and walked for an hour or so,
if no more than up and down the driveway, he could get
himself straightened out.

The blaze in the fireplace in the drawing room was
little more than a glimmer in the coals when he went past
the door.

A voice called to him: 'David, is that you?'

He spun around and went back to the door. A dark
figure was huddled on the sofa in front of the fireplace.

'Jonathon?' Latimer asked.

'Yes, it is. Why don't you keep me company. I'm an
old night owl and, in consequence, spend many lonely
hours. There's coffee on the table if you want it.'

Latimer walked to the sofa and sat down. Cups and a
carafe of coffee were on the table. He poured himself a
cup.

'You want a refill?' he asked Jonathon.

'If you please.' The older man held out his cup and
Latimer filled it. 'I drink a sinful amount of this stuff,'
said Jonathon. 'There's liquor in the cabinet. A dash of
brandy in the coffee, perhaps.'

'That sounds fine,' said Latimer. He crossed the room
and found the brandy, brought it back, pouring a dollop
into both cups.

They settled down and looked at one another. A nearly burned log in the fireplace collapsed into a mound of coals. In the flare of its collapse, Latimer saw the face of the other man – beard beginning to turn gray, an angular yet refined face, eyebrows that were sharp exlamation points.

'You're a confused young man,' said Jonathon.

'Extremely so,' Latimer confessed. 'I keep asking all the time why and who.'

Jonathon nodded. 'Most of us still do, I suppose. It's worst when you first come here, but you never quit. You keep on asking questions. You're frustrated and depressed when there are no answers. As time goes on, you come more and more to accept the situation and do less fretting about it. After all, life is pleasant here. All our needs are supplied, nothing is expected of us. We do much as we please. You, no doubt, have heard of Enid's theory that we are under observation by an alien race that has penned us here in order to study us.'

'Enid told me,' said Latimer, 'that she did not necessarily believe the theory, but regarded it as a nice idea, a neat and dramatic explanation of what is going on.'

'It is that, of course,' said Jonathon, 'but it doesn't stand up. How would aliens be able to employ the staff that takes such good care of us?'

'The staff worries me,' said Latimer. 'Are its members trapped here along with us?'

'No, they're not trapped,' said Jonathon. 'I'm certain they are employed, perhaps at very handsome salaries. The staff changes from time to time, one member leaving to be replaced by someone else. How this is accomplished we do not know. We've kept a sharp watch in the hope that we might learn and thus obtain a clue as to how we could get out of here, but it all comes to nothing. We try on occasions, not too obviously, to talk with the staff, but beyond normal civility, they will not talk with us. I have a sneaking suspicion, too, that there are some of us, perhaps including myself, who no longer try too hard. Once one has been here long enough to make peace with himself, the ease of our life grows upon us. It would be something we would be reluctant to part with. I can't imagine, personally, what I would do if I were turned out of here, back into the world that I have virtually forgotten. That is the vicious part of it – that our captivity is so attractive, we are inclined to fall in love with it.'

'But certainly in some cases there were people left behind – wives, husbands, children, friends.In my own case, no wife and only a few friends.'

'Strangely enough,' said Jonathon, 'where such ties existed, they were not too strong.'

'You mean only people without strong ties were picked?'

'No, I doubt that would have been the case. Perhaps among the kind of people who are here, there is no tendency to develop such strong ties.'

'Tell me what kind of people. You told me you are a philosopher and I know some of the others. What about Underwood?'

'A playwright. And a rather successful one before he came here.'

'Charlie? Jane?'

'Charlie is a cartoonist, Jane an essayist.'

'Essayist?'

'Yes, high social consciousness. She wrote rather telling articles for some of the so-called little magazines, even a few for more prestigious publications. Charlie was big in the Middle West. Worked for a small daily, but his cartoons were widely reprinted. He was building a reputation and probably would have been moving on to more important fields.'

'Then we're not all from around here. Not all from New England.'

No. Some of us, of course. Myself and you. The others are from other parts of the country.'

'All of us from what can be roughly called the arts. And from a wide area. How in the world would they – whoever they may be – have managed to lure all these people to this house? Because I gather we had to come ourselves, that none of us was seized and brought here.'

'I think you are right. I can't imagine how it was managed. Psychological management of some sort, I would assume, but I have no idea how it might be done.'

'You say you are a philosopher. Does that mean you taught philosophy?'

'I did at one time. But it was not a satisfactory job. Teaching those old dead philosophies to a group of youngsters who paid but slight attention was no bargain, I can tell you. Although, I shouldn't blame them, I suppose. Philosophy today is largely dead. It's primitive, outdated, the most of it. What we need is a new philosophy that will enable us to cope with the present world.'

'And you are writing such a philosophy?'

'Writing at it. I find that as time goes on, I get less and less done. I haven't the drive any longer. This life of ease, I suppose. Something's gone out of me. The anger, maybe. Maybe the loss of contact with the world I knew. No longer exposed to that world's conditions, I have lost the feel for it. I don't feel the need of protest, I've lost my sense of outrage, and the need for a new philosophy has become remote.'

'This business about the staff. You say that from time to time it changes.'

'It may be fairly simple to explain. I told you that we watch, but we can't have a watcher posted all the time. The staff, on the other hand, can keep track of us. Old staff members leave, others come in when we are somewhere else.'

'And supplies. They have to bring in supplies. That would not be as simple.'

Jonathon chuckled. 'You've really got your teeth in this.'

'I'm interested, dammit. There are questions about how the operation works and I want to know. How about the basement? Tunnels, maybe. Could they bring in staff and supplies through tunnels in the basement? I know that sounds cloak-and-dagger, but . . .'

'I suppose they could. If they did, we'd never know. The basement is used to store supplies and we're not welcome there. One of the staff, a burly brute who is a deaf-mute, or pretends to be, has charge of the basement. He lives down there, eats and sleeps down there, takes care of supplies.'

'It could be possible, then?'

'Yes,' said Jonathon. 'It could be possible.'

The fire had died down; only a few coals still blinked in the ash. In the silence that came upon them, Latimer heard the wind in the trees outside.

'One thing you don't know,' said Jonathon. 'You will find great auks down on the beach.'

'Great auks? That's impossible. They've been . . .'

'Yes, I now. Extinct for more than a hundred years. Also whales. Sometimes you can sight a dozen a day. Occasionally a polar bear.'

'Then that must mean . . .'

Jonathon nodded. 'We are somewhere in prehistoric North America. I would guess several thousand years into the past. We hear and, occasionally, see moose. There are a number of deer, once in a while woodland caribou. The bird life, especially the wildfowl, are here in incredible numbers. Good shooting if you ever have the urge. We have guns and ammunition.'

Dawn was beginning to break when Latimer went back to his room. He was bone-tired and now he could sleep. But before going to bed he stood for a time in front of the window overlooking the birch grove and the shore. A thin fog had moved off the water and everything had a faery, unrealistic cast.

Prehistoric North America, the philosopher had said, and if that was the case, there was little possibility of escape back to the world he knew. Unless one had the secret – or the technology – one did not move in time. Who, he wondered, could have cracked the technique of time transferral? And who, having cracked it, would use it for the ridiculous purpose of caging people in it?

There had been a man at MIT, he recalled, who had spent twenty years or more in an attempt to define time and gain some understanding of it. But that had been some years ago and he had dropped out of sight, or at least out of the news. From time to time there had been news stories (written for the most part with tongue firmly in cheek) about the study. Although, Latimer told himself, it need not have been the MIT man; there might have been other people engaged in similar studies who had escaped, quite happily, the attention of the press.

Thinking of it, he felt an excitement rising in him at the prospect of being in primitive North America, of being able to see the land as it had existed before white explorers had come – before the Norsemen or the Cabots or Cartier or any the others. Although there must be Indians about – it was funny that Jonathon had not mentioned Indians.

Without realizing that he had been doing so, he found that he had been staring at a certain birch clump. Two of the birch trees grew opposite one another, slightly behind but on opposite sides of a large boulder that he estimated at standing five feet high or so. And beyond the boulder, positioned slightly down the slope, but between the other two birch trees, was a third. It was not an unusual situation, he knew; birch trees often grew in clumps of three. There must have been some feature of the clump that had riveted his attention on it, but if that had been the case, he no longer was aware of it and it was not apparent now. Nevertheless, he remained staring at it, puzzled at what he had seen, if he had seen anything at all.

As he watched, a bird flew down from somewhere to light on the boulder. A songbird, but too far away for identification. Idly he watched the bird until it flew off the rock and disappeared.

Without bothering to undress, simply kicking off his shoes, he crossed the room to the bed and fell upon it, asleep almost before he came to rest upon it.

It was almost noon before he woke. He washed his face and combed his hair, not bothering to shave, and went stumbling down the stairs, still groggy from the befuddlement of having slept so soundly. No one else was in the house, but in the dining room a place was set and covered dishes remained upon the sideboard. He chose kidneys and scrambled eggs, poured a cup of coffee, and went back to the table. The smell of food triggered hunger, and after gobbling the plate of food, he went back for seconds and another cup of coffee.

When he went out through the rear door, there was no one in sight. The slope of birch stretched toward the coast. Off to his left, he heard two reports that sounded like shotguns. Perhaps someone out shooting duck or quail. Jonathon had said there was good hunting here.

He had to wend his way carefully through a confused tangle of boulders to reach the shore, with pebbles grating underneath his feet. A hundred yards away the inrolling breakers shattered themselves upon randomly scattered rocks, and even where he stood he felt the thin mist of spray upon his face.

Among the pebbles he saw a faint gleam and bent to see what it was. Closer to it, he saw that it was an agate –

tennis-ball size, its fractured edge, wet with spray, giving off a waxy, translucent glint. He picked it up and polished it, rubbing off the clinging bits of sand, remembering how as a boy he had hunted agates in abandoned gravel pits. Just beyond the one he had picked up lay another one, and a bit to one side of it, a third. Crouched, he hunched forward and picked up both of them. One was bigger than the first, the second slightly smaller. Crouched there, he looked at them, admiring the texture of them, feeling once again, after many years, the thrill he had felt as a boy at finding agates. When he had left home to go to college, he remembered there had been a bag full of them still cached away in one corner of the garage. He wondered what might have become of them.

A few yards down the beach, something waddled out from behind a cluster of boulders, heading for the water. A bird, it stood some thirty inches tall and had a fleeting resemblance to a penguin. The upper plumage was black, white below, a large white spot encircled its eye. Its small wings shifted as it waddled. The bill was sharp and heavy, a vicious striking weapon.

He was looking at, he knew, a great auk, a bird that up in his world had been extinct but which, a few centuries before, had been common from Cape Cod to far north in Canada. Cartier's seamen, ravenous for fresh meat as a relief from sea rations, had clubbed hundreds to death, eating some of them at once, putting what remained down in kegs with salt.

Behind the first great auk came another and then two more. Paying no attention to him, they waddled down across the pebbles to the water, into which they dived, swimming away.

Latimer remained in his crouch, staring at the birds in fascination. Jonathon had said he would find them on the beach, but knowing he would find them and actually seeing them, were two different things. Now he was convinced, as he had not been before, of exactly where he was.

Off to his left, the guns banged occasionally, but otherwise there were no signs of the others in the house. Far out across the water, a string of ducks went scuddling close above the waves. The pebbled beach held a sense of peace – the kind of peace, he thought, that men might have known long years ago when the earth was still largely empty of humankind, when there was still room for such peace to settle in and stay.

Squatting there upon the beach, he remembered the clump of birch and now, suddenly and without thinking of it, he knew what had attracted his attention to it – an aberration of perspective that his painter's eye had caught. Knitting his brow, he tried to remember exactly what it was that had made the perspective wrong, but whatever it had been quite escaped him now.

He glimpsed another agate and went to pick it up, and a little farther down the beach he found yet another one. This, he told himself, was an unworked, unpicked rock-hunters paradise. He put the agates in his pocket and continued down the beach. Spotting other agates, he did not pick them up. Later, at some other time, if need be, he could find hours of amusement hunting them.

When he climbed the beach and started up the slope, he saw that Jonathon was sitting in a chair on the veranda that ran across the back of the house. He climbed up to where he sat and settled down in another chair.

'Did you see an auk?' asked Jonathon.

'I saw four of them,' said Latimer.

'There are times,' said Jonathon, 'that the beach is crowded with them. Other times, you won't see one for days. Underwood and Charlie are off hunting woodcock. I suppose you heard them shooting. If they get back in time, we'll have woodcock for dinner. Have you ever eaten woodcock?'

'Only once. Some years ago. A friend and I went up to Nova Scotia to catch the early flight.'

'I guess that is right. Nova Scotia and a few other places now. Here I imagine you can find hunting of them wherever you can find alder swamps.'

'Where was everyone?' asked Latimer. 'When I got out of the sack and had something to eat, there was no one around.'

'The girls went out blackberrying,' said Jonathon. 'They do that often. Gives them something to do. It's getting a little late for blackberries, but there are some around. They got back in time to have blackberry pie tonight.' He smacked his lips. 'Woodcock and blackberry pie. I hope you are hungry.'

'Don't you ever think of anything but eating?'

'Lots of other things,' said Jonathon. 'Thing is, here you grab onto anything you can think about. It keeps you occupied. And I might ask you, are you feeling easier than you were last night? Got all the immediate questions answered?'

'One thing still bothers me,' said Latimer. 'I left my car parked outside the house. Someone is going to find it parked there and will wonder what has happened.'

'I think that's something you don't need to worry over,' said Jonathon. 'Whoever is engineering this business would have seen to it. I don't know, mind you, but I would guess that before morning your car was out of there and will be found, abandoned, some other place, perhaps a hundred miles away. The people we are dealing with would automatically take care of such small details. It wouldn't do to have too many incidents clustered about this house or in any other place. Your car will be found and you'll be missing and a hunt will be made for you. When you aren't found, you'll become just another one of the dozens of people who turn up missing every year.'

'Which leaves me to wonder,' said Latimer, 'how many of these missing people wind up in places such as this. It is probably this is not the only place where some of them are being trapped.'

'There is no way to know,' said Jonathon. 'People drop out for very many reasons.'

They sat silent for a time, looking out across the sweep of lawn. A squirrel went scampering down the slope. Far off, birds were calling. The distant surf was a hollow booming.

Finally, Latimer spoke. 'Last night, you told me we needed a new philosophy, that the old ones were no longer valid.'

'That I did,'said Jonathon. 'We are faced today with a managed society. We live by restrictive rules, we have been reduced to numbers – our Social Security numbers, our Internal Revenue Service numbers, the numbers on our credit cards, on our checking and savings accounts, on any number of other things. We are being dehumanized and, in most cases, willingly, because this numbers game may seem to make life easier, but most often because no one wants to bother to make a fuss about it. We have come to believe that a man who makes a fuss is antisocial. We are a flock of senseless chickens, fluttering and scurrying, cackling and squawking, but being shooed along in the way that others want us to go. The advertising agencies tell us what to buy, the public relations people tell us what to think, and even knowing this, we do not resent it. We sometimes damn the government when we work up the courage to damn anyone at all. But I am certain it is not the government we should be damning, but, rather, the world's business managers. We have seen the rise of multinational complexes that owe no loyalty to any government, that think and plan in global terms, that view the human populations as a joint labor corps – consumer group, some of which also may have investment potential. This is a threat, as I see it, against human free will and human dignity, and we need a philosophical approach that will enable us to deal with it.'

'And if you should write this philosophy,' said Latimer, 'it would pose a potential threat against the managers.'

'Not at first,' said Jonathon. 'Perhaps never. But it might have some influence over the years. It might start a trend of thinking. To break the grip the managers now hold would require something like a social revolution . . .'

'These men, these managers you are talking about – they would be cautious men, would they not, farseeing men? They would take no chances. They'd have too much at stake to take any chances at all.'

'You aren't saying . . .'

'Yes, I think I am. It is, at least, a thought.'

Jonathon said, 'I have thought of it myself but rejected it because I couldn't trust myself. It follows my bias too closely. And it doesn't make sense. If there were people they wanted to get out of the way, there'd be other ways to do it.'

'Not as safely,' said Latimer. 'Here there is no way we could be found. Dead, we would be found . . .'

'I wasn't thinking of killing.'

'Oh, well,' said Latimer, 'it was only a thought. Another guess.'

'There's one theory no one has told you, or I don't think they have. An experiment in sociology. Putting various groups of people together in unusual situations and measuring their reactions. Isolating them so there is no present-world influence to modify the impact of the situation.'

Latimer shook his head. 'It sounds like a lot of trouble and expense. More than the experiment would be worth.'

'I think so, too,' said Jonathon.

He rose from his chair. 'I wonder if you'd excuse me. I have the habit of stretching out for an hour or so before dinner. Sometimes I doze, other times I sleep, often I just lie there. But it is relaxing.'

'Go ahead,' said Latimer. 'We'll have plenty of time later to talk.'

For half an hour or more after Jonathon had left, he remained sitting in the chair, staring down across the lawn, but scarcely seeing it.

That idea about the managers being responsible for the situation, he told himself, made a ragged sort of sense. Managers, he thought with a smile – how easy it is to pick up someone else's lingo.

For one thing, the idea, if it worked, would be foolproof. Pick up the people you wanted out of the way and pop them into time, and after you popped them into time still keep track of them to be sure there were no slipups. And, at the same time, do them no real injustice, harm them as little as possible, keep a light load on your conscience, still be civilized.

There were two flaws, he told himself. The staff changed from time to time. That meant they must be rotated from here back to present time and they could be a threat. Some way would have had to be worked out to be sure they never talked, and given human nature, that would be a problem. The second flaw lay in the people who were here. The philosopher, if he had remained in present time, could have been a threat. But the rest of them? What threat could a poet pose? A cartoonist, maybe, perhaps a novelist, but a musician–composer – what threat could lie in music?

On the surface of it, however, it was not as insane as it

sounded if you happened not to be on the receiving end of it. The world could have been spared a lot of grief in the last few hundred years if such a plan had been operative, spotting potential troublemakers well ahead of the time they became a threat and isolating them. The hard part of such a plan – from where he sat, an apparently impossible part of it – would lie in accurately spotting the potential troublemakers before they began making trouble. Although that, he supposed, might be possible. Given the state of the art in psychology, it might be possible.

With a start, he realized that during all this time, without consciously being aware of it, he had been staring at the birch clump. And now he remembered another thing. Just before he had stumbled off to bed, he had seen a bird light on the boulder, sit there for a time, then lift itself into the air and disappear – not fly away, but disappear. He must have known this when he saw it, but been so fogged by need of sleep that the significance of it had not made an impression. Thinking back on it, he felt sure he was not mistaken. The bird had disappeared.

He reared out of the chair and strode down the slope until he stood opposite the boulder with the two trees flanking it and the other growing close behind it. He took one of the agates out of his pocket and tossed it carefully over the boulder, aimed so that it would strike the tree behind the rock. It did not strike the tree; he could not hear it fall to the ground. One by one, he tossed all the other agates as he had tossed the first. None of them hit the tree, none fell to the ground. To make sure, he went around the tree to the right and, crouching down, crawled behind the boulder. He carefully went over the ground. There were no agates there.

Shaken, his mind a seething turmoil of mingled doubt and wonder, he went back up the hill and sat in the chair again. Thinking the situation over as calmly as he could, there seemed to be no doubt that he had found a rift of some sort in – what would you call it? – the time continuum, perhaps. And if you wriggled through the rift or threw yourself through the rift, you'd not be here. He had thrown the agates and they were no longer here; they had gone elsewhere. But where would you go? Into some other time, most likely, and the best guess would seem to be back into the time from which he had been snatched. He had come from there to here, and if there were a rift in the time continuum, it would seem to be reasonable to believe the rift would lead back into present time again. There was a chance it wouldn't, but the chance seemed small, for only two times had been involved in the interchange.

And if he did go back, what could he do? Maybe not a lot, but he damn well could try. His first move would be to disappear, to get away from the locality and lose himself. Whoever was involved in this trapping scheme would try to find him, but he would make it his business to be extremely hard to find. Then, once he had done that, he would start digging, to ferret out the managers Jonathon had mentioned, or if not them, then whoever might be behind all this.

He could not tell the others here what he suspected. Inadvertently, one of them might tip off a staff member, or worse, might try to prevent him from doing what he meant to do, having no wish to change the even tenor of the life they enjoyed here.

When Underwood and Charlie came up the hill with their guns, their hunting coats bulging with the woodcock they had bagged, he went inside with them, where the others had gathered in the drawing room for a round of before-dinner drinks.

At dinner, there was, as Jonathon had said there would be, broiled woodcock and blackberry pie, both of which were exceptionally tasty, although the pie was very full of seeds.

After dinner, they collected once again before the fire and talked of inconsequential things. Later on Alice played and again it was Chopin.

In his room, he pulled a chair over to the window and sat there, looking out at the birch clump. He waited until he could hear no one stirring about, and then two more hours after that, to make sure all were safely in their beds, if not asleep. Then he went softly down the stairs and out the back door. A half-moon lighted the lawn so that he had little trouble locating the birch clump. Now that he was there, he was assailed by doubt. It was ridiculous to think, he told himself, what he had been thinking. He would climb up on the boulder and throw himself out toward the third tree that stood behind the boulder and he would tumble to the ground between the tree and boulder and nothing would have happened. He would trudge sheepishly up the slope again and go to bed, and after a time he would manage to forget what he had done and it would be as if he had never done it. And yet, he remembered, he had thrown the agates, and when he had looked, there had not been any agates.

He scrambled up the face of the boulder and perched cautiously on its rounded top. He put out his hands to grasp the third birch and save himself from falling. Then he launched himself toward the tree.

He fell only a short distance, but landed hard upon the ground. There had not been any birch to catch to break his fall.

A hot sun blazed down upon him. The ground beneath him was not a greasy lawn, but a sandy loam with no grass at all. There were some trees, but not any birches.

He scrambled to his feet and turned to look at the house. The hilltop stood bare; there was no house. Behind him, he could hear the booming of the surf as it battered itself to spray against the rocky coastline.

Thirty feet away, to his left, stood a massive poplar, its

leaves whispering in the wind that blew off the sea. Beyond it grew a scraggly pine tree and just down the slope, a cluster of trees that he thought were willows. The ground was covered – not too thickly covered, for rain-runneled soil showed through – by a growth of small ferns and other low-growing plants he could not identify.

He felt the perspiration starting from his body, running in rivulets from his armpits down his ribs – but whether from fear or sun, he did not know. For he was afraid, stiff and aching with the fear.

In addition to the poplar and the pine, low-growing shrubs were rooted in the ground among the ferns and other ground cover. Birds flew low, from one clump of shrubbery to another, chirping as they flew. From below him, their cries muted by the pounding of the surf, other birds were squalling. Gulls, he thought, or birds like gulls.

Slowly the first impact of the fear drained from him and he was able to move. He took a cautious step and then another and then was running toward the hilltop where the house should be, but wasn't.

Ahead of him, something moved and he skidded to a halt, poised to go around whatever had moved in the patch of shrubbery. A head poked out of the patch and stared at him with unblinking eyes. The nose was blunt and scaly and farther back the scales gave way to plates of armor. The thing mumbled at him disapprovingly and lurched forward a step or two, then halted.

It stood there, staring at him with its unblinking eyes. Its back was covered by overlapping plates. Its front legs were bowed. It stood four feet at the shoulder. It did not seem to be threatening; rather, it was curious.

His breath caught in his throat. Once, long ago, he had seen a drawing, an artist's conception, of this thing – not exactly like it, but very much the same. An anky, he thought – what was it? – an ankylosaurus, that was what it was, he realized, amazed that he should remember, an ankylosaurus. A creature that should have been dead for millions of years. But the caption had said six feet at the shoulder and fifteen feet long, and this one was nowhere near that big. A small one, he thought, maybe a young one, maybe a different species, perhaps a baby anky-whatever-the-hell-it-was.

Cautiously, almost on tiptoe, he walked around it, while it kept turning its head to watch him. It made no move toward him. He kept looking over his shoulder to be sure it hadn't moved. Herbivorous, he assured himself, an eater of plants – posing no danger to anything at all, equipped with armor plate to discourage the meat eaters that might slaver for its flesh. He tried hard to remember whether the caption had said it was herbivorous, but his mind, on that particular point, was blank.

Although, if it were here, there would be carnivores as well – and, for the love of God, what had he fallen into? Why hadn't he given more thought to the possibility that something like this might happen, that he would not, necessarily, automatically go back to present time, but might be shunted off into another time? And why, just as a matter of precaution, hadn't he armed himself before he left? There were high-caliber guns in the library and he could have taken one of them and a few boxes of ammunition if he had just thought about it.

He had failed to recognize the possibility of being dumped into a place like this, he admitted, because he had been thinking about what he wanted to happen, to the exclusion of all else, using shaky logic to convince himself that he was right. His wishful thinking, he now knew, had landed him in a place no sane man would choose.

He was back in the age of dinosaurs and there wasn't any house. He probably was the only human on the planet, and if his luck held out, he might last a day or two, but probably not much more than that. He knew he was going off the deep end again, thinking as illogically as he had been when he launched himself into the time rift. There might not be that many carnivores about, and if a man was observant and cautious and gave himself a chance to learn, he might be able to survive. Although the chances were that he was stuck here. There could be little hope that he could find another rift in time, and even if he did, there would be no assurance that it would take him to anything better than this. Perhaps, if he could find the point where he had emerged into this world, he might have a chance to locate the rift again, although there was no guarantee that the rift was a two-way rift. He stopped and looked around, but there was no way to know where he had first come upon this place. The landscape all looked very much the same.

The ankylosaurus, he saw, had come a little out of the shrub thicket and was nibbling quite contentedly at the ground cover. Turning his back upon it, he went trudging up the hill.

Before he reached the crest, he turned around again to have a look. The ankylosaurus was no longer around, or perhaps he did not know where to look for it. Down in the swale that had been the alder swamp where Underwood and Charlie had bagged the woodcock, a herd of small reptiles were feeding, browsing off low-growing shrubs and ground cover.

Along the skyline of the hill beyond which the herd was feeding, a larger creature lurched along on its hind legs, its body slanted upright at an angle, the shriveled forearms dangling at its side, its massive, brutal head jerking as it walked. The herd in the swale stopped their feeding, heads swiveling to look at the lurching horror. Then they ran, racing jerkily on skinny hind legs, like a flock of outsize, featherless chickens racing for their lives.

Latimer turned again and walked toward the top of the hill. The last slope was steep, steeper than he remembered it had been on that other, safer world. He was panting when he reached the crest, and he stopped a moment to regain his breath. Then, when he was breathing more easily, he turned to look toward the south.

Half-turned, he halted, amazed at what he saw – the last thing in the world that he had expected to see. Sited in the valley that lay between the hill on which he stood and the next headland to the south, was a building. Not a house, but a building. It stood at least thirty stories high and looked like an office building, its windows gleaming in the sun.

He sobbed in surprise and thankfulness, but even so, he did not begin to run toward it, but stood for a moment looking at it, as if he must look at it for a time to believe that it was there. Around it lay a park of grass and tastefully planted trees. Around the park ran a high wire fence and in the fence at the foot of the hill closest to him was a gate, beside which was a sentry box. Outside the sentry box stood two men who carried guns.

Then he was running, racing recklessly down the hill, running with great leaps, ducking thickets of shrubs. He stubbed his toe and fell, pinwheeling down the slope. He brought up against a tree and, the breath half-knocked out of him, got to his feet, gasping and wheezing. The men at the gate had not moved, but he knew that they had seen him; they were gazing up the hill toward him.

Moving at a careful, slower pace, he went on down the hill. The slope leveled off and he found a faint path that he followed toward the gate.

He came up to the two guards and stopped.

'You damn fool,' one of them said to him. 'What do you think you're doing, going out without a gun? Trying to get yourself killed?'

'There's been an old Tyranno messing around here for the last several days,' said the other guard. 'He was seen by several people. An old bastard like that could go on the prod at the sight of you and you wouldn't have a chance.'

The first guard jerked his rifle toward the gate. 'Get in there,' he said. 'Be thankful you're alive. If I ever catch you going out again without a gun, I'll turn you in, so help me.'

'Thank you, sir,' said Latimer.

He walked through the gate, following a path of crushed shells toward the front entrance of the office building. But now that he was there, safe behind the fence, the reaction began setting in. His knees were wobbly and he staggered when he walked. He sat down on a bench beneath a tree. He found that his hands were shaking and he held them hard against his thighs to stop the trembling.

How lucky could one get? he asked himself. And what did it mean? A house in the more recent past, an office building in this place that must be millions of years into the past. There had not been dinosaurs upon the earth for at least sixty million years. And the rift? How had the rift come about? Was it something that could occur naturally, or had it come about because someone was manipulating time? Would such rifts come when someone, working deliberately, using techniques of which there was no public knowledge, was putting stress upon the web of time? Was it right to call time a web? He decided that it made no difference, that the terminology was not of great importance.

An office building, he thought. What did an office building mean? Was it possible that he had stumbled on the headquarters of the project/conspiracy/program that was engaged in the trapping of selected people in the past? Thinking of it, the guess made sense. A cautious group of men could not take the chance of operating such an enterprise in present time, where it might be nosed out by an eager-beaver newsman or a governmental investigation or by some other means. Here, buried in millions of years of time, there would be little chance of someone unmasking it.

Footsteps crunched on the path and Latimer looked up. A man in sports shirt and flannels stood in front of him.

'Good morning, sir,' said Latimer.

The man asked, 'Could you be David Latimer, by any chance?'

'I could be, said Latimer.

'I thought so. I don't remember seeing you before. I was sure I knew everyone. And the guards reported . . .'

'I arrived only an hour or so ago.'

'Mr Gale wanted to see you as soon as you arrived.'

'You mean you were expecting me?'

'Well, we couldn't be absolutely sure,' said the other. 'We are glad you made it.'

Latimer got off the bench and the two of them walked together to the front entrance, climbed the steps, and went through the door. They walked through a deserted lounge, then into a hallway flanked by numbered doors with no names upon them. Halfway down the hall, the man with Latimer knocked at one of the doors.

'Come in,' a voice said.

The man opened the door and stuck his head in. 'Mr Latimer is here,' he said. 'He made it.'

'That is fine,' said the voice. 'I am glad he did. Please show him in.'

The man stepped aside to allow Latimer to enter, then stepped back into the hall and closed the door. Latimer stood alone, facing the man across the room.

'I'm Donovan Gale,' said the man, rising from his desk and coming across the room. He held out his hand

and Latimer took it. Gale's grasp was a friendly corporate handshake.

'Let's sit over here,' he said, indicating a davenport. 'It seems to me we may have a lot to talk about.'

'I'm interested in hearing what you have to say,' said Latimer.

'I guess both of us are,' said Gale. 'Interested in what the other has to say, I mean.'

They sat down on opposite ends of the davenport, turning to face one another.

'So you are David Latimer,' said Gale. 'The famous painter.'

'Not famous,' said Latimer. 'Not yet. And it appears now that I may never be. But what I don't understand is how you were expecting me.'

'We knew you'd left Auk House.'

'So that is what you call it. Auk House.'

'And we suspected you would show up here. We didn't know exactly where, although we hoped that it would be nearby. Otherwise you never would have made it. There are monsters in those hills. Although, of course, we could not be really sure that you would wind up here. Would you mind telling us how you did it?'

Latimer shook his head. 'I don't believe I will. Not right now, at least. Maybe later on when I know more about your operation. And now a question for you. Why me? Why an inoffensive painter who was doing no more than trying to make a living and a reputation that might enable him to make a better living?'

'I see,' said Gale, 'that you have it figured out.'

'Not all of it,' said Latimer. 'And, perhaps, not all of it correctly. But I resent being treated as a bad guy, as a potential threat of some sort. I haven't got the guts or the motive to be a bad guy. And Enid, for Christ's sake. Enid is a poet. And Alice. All Alice does is play a good piano.'

'You're talking to the wrong men,' Gale told him.

'Breen could tell you that, if you can get him to tell you. I'm only personnel.'

'Who is Breen?'

'He's head of the evaluation team.'

'Those are the ones who figure out who is going to be picked up and tossed into time.'

'Yes, that is the idea, crudely. There's a lot more to it than that. There is a lot of work done here. Thousands of newspapers and other periodicals to be read to spot potential subjects. Preliminary psychological determinations. Then it's necessary to do further study back on prime world. Further investigation of potential subjects. But no one back there really knows what is going on. They're just hired to do jobs now and then. The real work goes on here.'

'Prime world is present time? Your old world and mine?'

'Yes. If you think, however, of prime world as present time, that's wrong. That's not the way it is. We're not dealing with time, but with alternate worlds. The one you just came from is a world where everything else took place exactly as it did in prime world, with one exception – man never evolved. There are no men there and never will be. Here, where we are now, something more drastic occurred. Here the reptiles did not become extinct. The Cretaceous never came to an end, the Cenozoic never got started. The reptiles are still the dominant species and the mammals still are secondary.'

'You're taking a chance, aren't you, in telling me all this.'

'I don't think so,' said Gale. 'You're not going anywhere. There are none of us going anywhere. Once we sign up for this post, we know there's not any going back. We're stuck here. Unless you have a system . . .'

'No system. I was just lucky.'

'You're something of an embarrassment to us,' said

Gale. 'In the years since the program has been in operation, nothing like this has happened at any of the stations. We don't know what to make of it and we don't quite know what to do with you. For the moment, you'll stay on as a guest. Later on, if it is your wish, we could find a place for you. You could become a member of the team.'

'Right at the moment,' said Latimer, 'that holds no great attraction for me.'

'That's because you aren't aware of the facts, nor of the dangers. Under the economic and social systems that have been developed in prime world, the great mass of mankind has never had it so good. There are ideological differences, of course, but there is some hope that they eventually can be ironed out. There are underprivileged areas; this cannot be denied. But one must also concede that their only hope lies in their development by free-world business interests. So-called big-business interests are the world's one hope. With the present economic structure gone, the entire world would go down into another Dark Age, from which it would require a thousand years or more to recover, if recovery, in fact, were possible at all.'

'So to protect your precious economic structure, you place a painter, a poet, a musician into limbo.'

Gale made a despairing gesture with his hands. 'I have told you I can't supply the rationale on that. You'll have to see Breen if he has the time to see you. He's a very busy man.'

'I would imagine that he might be.'

'He might even dig out the files and tell you,' said Gale. 'As I say, you're not going anywhere. You can pose no problem now. You are stuck with us and we with you. I suppose that we could send you back to Auk House, but that would be undesirable, I think. It would only upset the people who are there. As it is, they'll probably figure that you simply wandered off and got killed by a bear or bitten by a rattlesnake, or drowned in a swamp. They'll look for you and when they don't find you, that will be it. You only got lost; they'll never consider for a moment that you escaped. I think we had better leave it at that. Since you are here and, given time, would nose out the greater part of our operation, we have no choice but to be frank with you. Understandably, however, we'd prefer that no one outside this headquarters knew.'

'Back at Auk House, there was a painting of mine hanging in my room.'

'We thought it was a nice touch,' said Gale. 'A sort of friendly thing to do. We could bring it here.'

'That wasn't why I asked,' said Latimer. 'I was wondering – did the painting's subject have something to do with what you did to me? Were you afraid that I would go on painting pictures pointing up the failures of your precious economic structure?'

Gale was uncomfortable. 'I couldn't say,' he said.

'I was about to say that if such is the case, you stand on very flimsy ground and carry a deep guilt complex.'

'Such things are beyond me,' said Gale. 'I can't even make a comment.'

'And this is all you want of me? To stand in place? To simply be a guest of all these big-hearted corporations?'

'Unless you want to tell us how you got here.'

'I have told you that I won't do that. Now now. I suppose if you put me to the torture . . .'

'We wouldn't torture you,' said Gale. 'We are civilized. We regret some of the things that we must do, but we do not flinch from duty. And not the duty to what you call big-hearted corporations, but to all humankind. Man has a good thing going; we can't allow it to be undermined. We're not taking any chances. And now, perhaps I should call someone to show you to your room. I take it you got little sleep last night.'

Latimer's room was on one of the topmost floors and was larger and somewhat more tastefully furnished than the room at Auk House. From a window, he saw that the conformation of the coastline was much the same as it had been at Auk House. The dirty gray of the ocean stretched off to the east and the surf still came rolling in to break upon the boulders. Some distance off shore, a school of long-necked creatures were cavorting in the water. Watching them more closely, Latimer made out that they were catching fish. Scattered reptilian monstrosities moved about in the hills that ran back from the sea, some of them in small herds, some of them alone. Dwarfed by distance, none of them seemed unusually large. The trees, he saw, were not a great deal different from the ones he had known. The one thing that was wrong was the lack of grass.

He had been a victim of simplistic thinking in be-lieving, he told himself, that when he threw himself into the rift he would be carried to present time or prime world or whatever one might call it. In the back of his mind, as well, although he had not really dared to think it, had been the idea that if he could get back to the real world, he could track down the people who were in-volved and put a stop to it.

There was no chance of that now, he knew, and there never had been. Back on prime world, there would be no evidence that would stand up, only highly paid lackeys who performed necessary chores. Private investigators, shady operators like the Boston realtor and the Campbell who had listed Auk House for sale or rent. Undoubtedly, the sign announcing the house was available was posted only when a potential so-called customer would be driving past. Campbell would have been paid well, perhaps in funds that could not be traced, for the part he played, offering the house and then, perhaps, driving off the car left behind by the customer. He took some risks, certainly, but they were minimal. Even should he have been apprehended, there would be no way in which he could be tied into the project. He, himself, would have had no inkling of the project. A few men in prime world would have to know, of course, for some sort of communications had to be maintained between this operations center and prime world. But the prime-world men, undoubtedly, would be solid citizens, not too well known, all beyond suspicion or reproach. They would be very careful against the least suspicion, and the communications between them and this place must be of a kind that could not be traced and would have no record.

Those few upright men, perhaps a number of hired hands who had no idea of what was being done, would be the only ones in prime world who would play any part in the project. The heart of the operation was in this building. Here the operations were safe. There was no way to get at them. Gale had not even bothered to deny what was being done, had merely referred him to Breen for any further explanation. And Breen, should he talk with him, probably would make no denial, either.

And here he stood, David Latimer, artist, the one man outside the organization who, while perhaps not realizing the full scope of the project, still knew what was happening. Knew and could do nothing about it. He ran the facts he had so far acquired back and forth across his mind, seeking some chink of weakness, and there seemed to be none.

Silly, he thought, one man pitting himself against a group that held the resources of the earth within its grasp, a group at once ruthless and fanatical, that commanded as its managers the best brains of the planet, arrogant in its belief that what was good for the group was good for everyone, brooking no interference, alert to even the slightest threat, even to imagined threat.

Silly, perhaps absurdly quixotic – and, yet, what could

he do? To save his own self-respect, to pay even lip service to the dignity of humanity, he must make at least a token effort, even knowing that the possibility of his accomplishing anything was very close to zero.

Say this much for them, he thought, they were not cruel men. In many ways, they were compassionate. Their imagined enemies were neither killed nor confined in noisome prisons, as had been the case with historic tyrants. They were held under the best of circumstances, all their needs were supplied, they were not humiliated. Everything was done to keep them comfortable and happy. The one thing that had been taken from them was their freedom of choice.

But man, he thought, had fought for bitter centuries for that very freedom. It was not something that should be lightly held or easily relinquished.

All this, at the moment, he thought, was pointless. If he should be able to do anything at all, it might not be until after months of observation and learning. He could remain in the room for hours, wallowing in his doubt an incompetency, and gain not a thing by it. It was time to begin to get acquainted with his new surroundings.

The parklike grounds surrounding the buildings were ringed by the fence, twelve feet high or more, with a four-foot fence inside it. There were trees and shrubs and beds of flowers and grass – the only grass he had seen since coming here, a well-tended greensward.

Paths of crushed shell ran among the trees and underneath them was a coolness and a quiet. A few gardeners worked in flower beds and guards stood at the distant gate, but otherwise there were few people about. Probably it was still office hours; later on, there might be many people.

He came upon the man sitting on the bench when the walk curved sharply around a group of head-high shrubbery. Latimer stopped, and for a moment they regarded one another as if each was surprised at the appearance of the other.

Then the man on the bench said, with a twinkle in his eye, 'It seems that the two of us are the only ones who have no tasks on this beautiful afternoon. Could you be, possibly, the refugee from Auk House?'

'As a matter of fact, I am,' said Latimer. 'My name is David Latimer, as if you didn't know.'

'Upon my word,' said the other, 'I didn't know your name. I had only heard that someone had escaped from Auk House and had ended up with us. News travels swiftly here. The place is a rumor mill. There is so little of consequence that happens that once some notable event does occur, it is chewed to tiny shreds.

'My name, by the way, is Horace Sutton and I'm a paleontologist. Can you imagine a better place for a paleontologist to be?'

'No, I can't,' said Latimer.

'Please share this bench with me,' invited Sutton. 'I take it there is nothing of immediate urgency that requires your attention.'

'Not a thing,' said Latimer. 'Nothing whatsoever.'

'Well, that is fine,' said Sutton. 'We can sit and talk a while or stroll around for a bit, however you may wish. Then, as soon as the sun gets over the yardarm, if by that time you're not totally disenchanted with me, we can indulge ourselves in some fancy drinking.'

Sutton's hair was graying and his face was lined, but there was something youthful about him that offset the graying hair and lines.

Latimer sat down and Sutton said to him, 'What do you think of this layout? A charming place, indeed. The tall fence, as you may have guessed, is electrified, and the lower fence keeps stupid people such as you and I from blundering into it. Although, there have been times I have been glad the fence is there. Comes a time when a carnivore or two scents the meat in here and is intent upon a feast, you are rather glad it's there.'

'Do they gather often? The carnivores, I mean.'

'Not as much as they did at one time. After a while, the knowledge of what to keep away from sinks into even a reptilian brain.'

'As a paleontologist you study the wildlife here.'

'For the last ten years,' said Sutton. 'I guess a bit less time than that. It was strange at first; it still seems a little strange. A paleontologist, you understand, ordinarily works with bones and fossil footprints and other infuriating evidence that almost tells you what you want to know, but always falls short.

'Here there is another problem. From the viewpoint of prime world, many of the reptiles, including the dinosaurs, died out sixty-three million years ago. Here they did not die out. As a result, we are looking at them not as they were millions of years ago, but as they are after millions of additional years of evolutionary development. Some of the old species have disappeared, others have evolved into something else in which you can see the traces of their lineage, and some entirely new forms have arisen.'

'You sound as if your study of them is very dedicated,' said Latimer. 'Under other circumstances, you would probably be writing a book . . .'

'But I am writing a book,' said Sutton. 'I am hard at work on it. There is a man here who is very clever at drawing and he is making diagrams for me and there will be photographs . . .'

'But what's the point?' asked Latimer. 'Who will publish it? When will it be published? Gale told me that no one ever leaves here, that there is no going back to prime world.'

'That is right,' said Sutton. 'We are exiled from prime world. I often think of us as a Roman garrison stationed, say, on Britain's northern border or in the wilds of Dacia, with the understanding that we'll not be going back to Rome.'

'But that means your book won't be published. I suppose it could be transmitted back to prime world and be printed there, but the publishing of it would destroy the secrecy of the project.'

'Exactly how much do you know about the project?' Sutton asked.

'Not much, perhaps. Simply the purpose of it — the trapping of people in time — no, not time, I guess. Alternate worlds, rather.'

'Then you don't know the whole of it?'

'Perhaps I don't,' said Latimer.

'The matter of removing potentially dangerous personnel from prime world,' said Sutton, 'is only part of it. Surely if you have thought of it at all, you could see other possibilities.'

'I haven't had time to think too deeply on it,' said Latimer. 'No time at all, in fact. You don't mean the exploitation of these other worlds?'

'It's exactly what I mean,' said Sutton. 'It is so obvious, so logical. Prime world is running out of resources. In these worlds, they lie untouched. The exploitation of the alternate worlds not only would open new resources, but would provide employment, new lands for colonization, new space for expansion. It is definitely a better idea than this silly talk you hear about going off into outer space to find new worlds that could be colonized.'

'Then why all the mummery of using it to get rid of potential enemies?'

'You sound as if you do not approve of this part of the project.'

'I'm not sure I approve of any of it and certainly not of picking up people and stashing them away. You seem to

ignore the fact that I was one of those who was picked up
and stashed away. The whole thing smells of paranoia.
For the love of God, the big business interests of prime
world have so solid a grip on the institutions of the Earth
and, in large part, on the people of the Earth, that there
is no reason for the belief that there is any threat against
them.'

'But they do take into account,' said Sutton, 'the possibility of such threats rising in the years to come, probably based upon events that could be happening right
now. They have corps of psychologists who are pursuing
studies aimed against such possibilities, corps of econ-
omists and political scientists who are looking at possible
future trends that might give rise to antibusiness
reactions. And, as you know, they are pinpointing
certain specific areas and peoples who could contribute,
perhaps unwittingly, either now or in the future, to undesirable reactions. But, as I understand it, they are
hopeful that if they can forestall the trends that would
bring about such reactions for a few centuries, then the
political, the economic, and the social climates will be so
solidly committed in their favor, that they can go ahead
with the exploitation of some of the alternate worlds.
They want to be sure before they embark on it, however,
that they won't have to keep looking over their
shoulders.'

'But hundreds of years! All the people who are engaged in this project will have been long dead by then.'

'You forget that a corporation can live for many
centuries. The corporations are the driving force here.
And, in the meantime, those who work in the project
gain many advantages. It is worth their while.'

'But they can't go back to Earth – back to prime
world, that is.'

'You are hung up on prime world,' said Sutton. 'By
working in the project, you are showered with

advantages that prime world could never give you. Work in the project for twenty years, for example, and at the age of fifty – in some cases, even earlier – you can have a wide choice of retirements – an estate somewhere on Auk world, a villa on a paradise world, a hunting lodge in another world where there is a variety of game that is unbelievable. With your family, if you have one, with servants, with your every wish fulfilled. Tell me, Mr Latimer, could you do as well if you stayed on prime world? I've listed only a few possibilities; there are many others.'

'Gale told me it would be possible to send me back to Auk House. So people can move around these alternate worlds, but not back to prime world?'

'That is right. Supplies for all the worlds are transported to this world and from here sent out to other stations.'

'But how? How is this done?'

'I have no idea. There is an entire new technology involved. Once I had thought it would be matter transmitters, but I understand it's not. Certain doors exist. Doors with quote marks around them. I suppose there is a corps of elite engineers who knew, but would suspect that no one else does.'

'You spoke of families.'

'There are families here.'

'But I didn't see . . .'

'The kids are in school. There aren't many people about right now. They'll be showing up at the cocktail hour. A sort of country-club routine here. That's why I like to get up early. Not many are about. I have this park to myself.'

'Sutton, you sound as if you like this setup.'

'I don't mind it,' Sutton said. 'It's far preferable to what I had in prime world. There my reputation had been ruined by a silly dispute I fell into with several of my colleagues. My wife died. My university let me stay on in sufferance. So when I was offered a decent job . . .'

'Not telling you what kind of job?'

'Well, no, not really. But the conditions of employment sounded good and I would be in sole charge of the investigation that was in prospect. To be frank with you, I jumped at it.'

'You must have been surprised.'

'In fact, I was. It took a while to reconcile myself to the situation.'

'But why would they want a paleontologist?'

'You mean, why would money-grabbing, cynical corporations want a paleontologist?'

'I guess that's what I mean.'

'Look, Latimer – the men who make up the corporations are not monsters. They saw here the need for a study of a truly unique world – a continuation of the Cretaceous, which has been, for years, an intriguing part of the planet's history. They saw it as a contribution to human knowledge. My book, when it is published, will show this world at a time before the impact of human exploitation fell upon it.'

'When your book is published?'

'When it is safe to make the announcement that alternate worlds have been discovered and are being opened for colonization. I'll never see the book, of course, but nevertheless, I take some pride in it. Here I have found confirmation for my stand that brought about condemnation by my colleagues. Fuzzy thinking, they said, but they were the fuzzy thinkers. This book will vindicate me.'

'And that's important? Even after you are dead?'

'Of course it is important. Even after I am dead.'

Sutton looked at his watch. 'I think,' he said, 'it may be time now. It just occurred to me. Have you had anything to eat?'

'No,' said Latimer. 'I hadn't thought of it before. But I am hungry.'

'There'll be snacks in the bar,' said Sutton. 'Enough to hold you until dinner.'

'One more question before we leave,' said Latimer. 'You said the reptiles showed some evolutionary trends. In what direction? How have they changed?'

'In many ways,' said Sutton. 'Bodily changes, of course. Perhaps ecological changes as well – behavioral changes, although I can't be sure of that. I can't know what their behavior was before. Some of the bigger carnivores haven't changed at all. Perhaps a bit more ability in a number of cases. Their prey may have become faster, more alert, and the carnivores had to develop a greater agility or starve. But the most astonishing change is in intelligence. There is one species, a brand-new species so far as I know, that seems to have developed a pronounced intelligence. If it is intelligence, it is taking a strange direction. It's hard to judge correctly. You must remember that of all the stupid things that ever walked the earth, some of the dinosaurs ranked second to none. They didn't have a lick of sense.'

'You said intelligence in a strange direction.'

'Let me try to tell you. I've watched these jokers for hours on end. I'm almost positive that they handle herds of herbivores – herbivorous reptiles, that is. They don't run around them like sheepdogs manage sheep, but I am sure they do control them. There are always a few of them watching the herds, and while they're watching them, the herds do no straying – they stay together like a flock of sheep tended by dogs. They move off in orderly fashion when there is need to move to a new pasture. And every once in a while, a few members of the herd with detach themselves and go ambling off to a place where others of my so-called intelligent dinosaurs are hanging out, and there they are killed. They walk in to be slaughtered. I can't get over the feeling that the herbivores are meat herds, the livestock of the intelligence species. And another thing. When carnivores roam in, these intelligent jokers shag them out of there. Not by chasing them or threatening them. Just by moving out where they can be seen. Then they sit down, and after the carnivores have looked them over, the carnivores seem to get a little jittery, and after a short time they move off.'

'Hypnotism? Some sort of mental power?'

'Possibly.'

'That wouldn't have to be intelligence. It could be no no more than an acquired survival trait.'

'Somehow I don't think so. Other than watching herds and warning off carnivores – if that is what they're doing – they sit around a lot among themselves. Like a bunch of people talking. That's the impression I get, that they are talking. None of the social mannerisms that are seen among primates – no grooming, horseplay, things like that. There seems to be little personal contact – no touching, no patting, no stroking. As if none of this were needed. But they dance. Ritualistic dancing of some sort. Without music. Nothing to make music with. They have no artifacts. They haven't got the hands that could fashion artifacts. Maybe they don't need tools or weapons or musical instruments. Apparently they have certain sacred spots. Places where they go, either singly or in small groups, to meditate or worship. I know of one such place; there may be others. No idols, nothing physical to worship. A secluded spot. Seemingly a special place. They have been using it for years. They have worn a path to it, a path trod out through the centuries. They seem to have no form of worship, no rituals that must be observed. They simply go and sit there. At no special time. There are no Sundays in this world. I suspect they go only when they feel the need of going.'

'It is a chilling thought,' said Latimer.

'Yes, I suppose it is.'

He looked at his watch again. 'I am beginning to feel the need of that drink,' he said. 'How about you?'

'Yes,' said Latimer, 'I could do with one.'

And now, he told himself, he had a few more of the answers. He knew how the staff at Auk House was changed, where the supplies came from. Everything and everyone, apparently, was channeled and routed from this operations center. Prime world, from time to time, furnished supplies and personnel and then the rest was handled here.

He found himself puzzled by Sutton's attitude. The man seemed quite content, bore no resentment over being exiled here. They are not monsters, he had said, implying that the men in this operation were reasonable and devoted men working in the public interest. He was convinced that someday his book would be published, according him posthumous vindication. There had been, as well, Latimer remembered, Enid's poems and Dorothy's novel. Had the poems and the novel been published back in prime world, perhaps under pseudonyms, works so excellent that it had been deemed important that they not be lost?

And what about the men who had done the research that had resulted in the discovery of the alternate worlds and had worked out the technique of reaching and occupying them? Not still on prime world, certainly; they would pose too great a danger there. Retired, perhaps, to estates on some of the alternate worlds.

They walked around one of the clumps of trees with which the park was dotted, and from a distance Latimer heard the sound of children happy at their play.

'School is out,' said Sutton. 'Now it's the children's hour.'

'One more thing,' said Latimer, 'if you don't mind.

One more question. On all these other alternate worlds you mention, are there any humans native to those worlds? Is it possible there are other races of men?'

'So far as I know,' said Sutton, 'man rose only once, on prime world. What I have told you is not the entire story, I imagine. There may be much more to it. I've been too busy to attempt to find out more. All I told you are the things I have picked up in casual conversation. I do not know how many other alternate worlds have been discovered, nor on how many of them stations have been established. I do know that on Auk world there are several stations other than Auk House.'

'By stations, you mean the places where they put the undesirables.'

'You put it very crudely, Mr Latimer, but yes, you are quite right. On the matter of humans arising elsewhere, I think it's quite unlikely. It seems to me that it was only by a combination of a number of lucky circumstances that man evolved at all. When you take a close look at the situation, you have to conclude that man had no right to expect to evolve. He is a sort of evolutionary accident.'

'And intelligence? Intelligence rose on prime world, and you seem to have evidence that it has risen here as well. Is intelligence something that evolution may be aiming at and will finally achieve, in whatever form on whatever world? How can you be sure it has not risen on Auk world? At Auk House, only a few square miles have been explored. Perhaps not a great deal more around the other stations.'

'You ask impossible questions,' said Sutton shortly. 'There is no way I can answer them.'

They had reached a place from which a full view of the headquarters building was possible and now there were many people – men and women walking about or sunning themselves, stretched out on the grass, people sitting on terraces in conversational groups, while children ran gaily, playing a childish game.

Sutton, who had been walking ahead of Latimer, stopped so quickly that Latimer, with difficulty, averted bumping into him.

Sutton pointed. 'There they are,' he said.

Looking in the direction of the pointing finger, Latimer could see nothing unusual. 'What? Where?' he asked.

'On top the hill, just beyond the northern gate.'

After a moment Latimer saw them, a dozen squatting creatures on top of the hill down which, a few hours ago, he had run for the gate and safety. They were too distant to be seen clearly, but they had a faintly reptilian look and they seemed to be coal-black, but whether naturally black or black because of their silhouetted position, he could not determine.

'The ones I told you about,' said Sutton. 'It's nothing unusual. They often sit and watch us. I suspect they are as curious about us as we are about them.'

'The intelligences?' asked Latimer.

'Yes, that is right,' said Sutton.

Someone, some distance off, cried in a loud voice – no words that Latimer could make out, but a cry of apprehension, a bellow of terror. Then there were other cries, different people taking up the cry.

A man was running across the park, heading for its northeast corner, running desperately, arms pumping back and forth, legs a blur of scissoring speed. He was so far off that he looked like a toy runner, heading for the four-foot fence that stood inside the higher fence. Behind him were other runners, racing in an attempt to head him off and pull him down.

'My God, it's Breen,' gasped Sutton. His face had turned to gray. He started forward, in a stumbling run. He opened his mouth to shout, but all he did was gasp.

The running man came to the inner fence and cleared it with a leap. The nearest of his pursuers was many feet behind him.

Breen lifted his arms into the air, above his head. He slammed into the electrified fence. A flash blotted him out. Flickering tongues of flame ran along the fence – bright and sparkling, like the flaring of fireworks. Then the brightness faded and on the fence hung a black blot that smoked greasily and had a fuzzy, manlike shape.

A hush, like an indrawn breath, came upon the crowd. Those who had been running stopped running and, for a moment, held their places. Then some of them, after that moment, ran again, although some of them did not, and the voice took up again, although now there was less shouting.

When he looked, Latimer saw that the hilltop was empty; the dinosaurs that had been there were gone. There was no sign of Sutton.

So it was Breen, thought Latimer, who hung there on the fence. Breen, head of the evaluation team, the one man, Gale had said, who could tell him why he had been lured to Auk House. Breen, the man who pored over psychological evaluations, who was acquainted with the profile of each suspected personage, comparing those profiles against economic charts, social diagnostic indices, and God knows what else, to enable him to make the decision that would allow one man to remain in prime world as he was, another to be canceled out.

And now, thought Latimer, it was Breen who had been canceled out, more effectively than he had canceled any of the others.

Latimer had remained standing where he had been when Sutton and he had first sighted the running Breen, had stood because he could not make up his mind what he should do, uncertain of the relationship that he held or was expected to assume with those other persons who

were still milling about, many of them perhaps as uncertain as he of what they should do next.

He began to feel conspicuous because of just standing
there, although at the same time he was certain no one
noticed him, or if they did notice him, almost immediately
dismissed him from their thoughts.

He and Sutton had been on their way to get a drink
when it had all happened, and thinking of that, Latimer
realized he could use a drink. With this in mind, he
headed for the building. Few noticed him, some even
brushing against him without notice; others spoke
noncommittal greetings, some nodded briefly as one nods
to someone of whose identity he is not certain.

The lounge was almost empty. Three men sat at a table
in one corner, their drinks before them; a woman and a
man were huddled in low-voiced conversation on a corner
of a davenport; another man was at the self-service bar,
pouring himself a drink.

Latimer made his way to the bar and picked up a glass.

The man who was there said to him, 'You must be new
here; I don't remember seeing you about.'

'Just today,' said Latimer. 'Only a few hours ago.'

He found the Scotch and his brand was not among the
bottles. He selected his second choice and poured a
generous serving over ice. There were several trays of
sandwiches and other snack items. He found a plate, put
two sandwiches on it.

'What do you make of Breen?' asked the other man.

'I don't know,' said Latimer. 'I never met the man.
Gale mentioned him to me.'

'Three,' said the other man. 'Three in the last four
months. There is something wrong.'

'All on the fence?'

'No, not on the fence. This is the first on the fence. One
jumped, thirteen stories. Christ, what a mess! The other
hanged himself.'

The man walked off and joined another man who had just come into the lounge. Latimer stood alone, plate and glass in hand. The lounge still was almost empty. No one was paying the slightest attention to him. Suddenly he felt a stranger, unwanted. He had been feeling this all the time, he knew, but in the emptiness of the lounge, the feeling of unwantedness struck with unusual force. He could sit down at a table or in one of a group of chairs or on the end of an unoccupied sofa, wait for someone to join him. He recoiled from the thought. He didn't want to meet these people, talk with them. For the moment, he wanted none of them.

Shrugging, he put another sandwich on the plate, picked up the bottle, and filled his glass to the top. Then he walked out into the hallway and took the elevator to his floor.

In his room, he selected the most comfortable chair and sat down in it, putting the plate of sandwiches on a table. He took a long drink and put down the glass.

'They can all go to hell,' he told himself.

He sensed his fragmented self pulling back together, all the scattered fragments falling back into him again, making him whole again, his entire self again. With no effort at all, he wiped out Breen and Sutton, the events of the last hours, until he was simply a man seated comfortably in his room.

So great a power, he thought, so great and secret. Holding one world in thrall, planning to hold others. The planning, the foresight, the audacity. Making certain that when they moved into the other worlds, there would be no silly conservationists yapping at their heels, no environmentalist demanding environmental impact statements, no deluded visionaries crying out in protest against monopolies. Holding steadily in view the easy business ethic that had held sway in that day when arrogant lumber barons had built mansions such as Auk House.

Latimer picked up the glass and had another drink. The glass, he saw, was less than half full. He should have carried off the bottle, he thought; no one would have noticed. He reached for a sandwich and munched it down, picked up a second one. How long had it been since he had eaten? He glanced at his watch and knew, even as he did, that the time it told might not be right for this Cretaceous world. He puzzled over that, trying to figure out if there might be some time variance between one world and another. Perhaps there wasn't – logically there shouldn't be – but there might be factors . . . he peered closely at the watch face, but the figures wavered and the hands would not stay in line. He had another drink.

He woke to darkness, stiff and cramped, wondering where he was. After a moment of confusion, he remembered where he was, all the details of the last two days tumbling in upon him, at first in scattered pieces, then subtly arranging themselves and interlocking into a pattern of reality.

He had fallen asleep in the chair. The moonlight pouring through the window showed the empty glass, the plate with half a sandwich still upon it, standing on the table at his elbow. The place was quiet; there was no noise at all. It must be the middle of the night, he thought, and everyone asleep. Or might it be that there was no one else around, that in some strange way, for some strange reason, the entire headquarters had been evacuated, emptied of all life? Although that, he knew, was unreasonable.

He rose stiffly from the chair and walked to the window. Below him, the landscape was pure silver, blotched by deep shadows. Somewhere just beyond the fence, he caught a sense of movement, but was unable to make out what it was. Some small animal, perhaps, prowling about. There would be mammals here, he was

sure, the little skitterers, frightened creatures that were
hard-pressed to keep out of the way, never having had
the chance to evolve as they had back in prime world
when something had happened millions of years before
to sweep the world clean of its reptilian overlords,
creating a vacuum into which they could expand.

The silver world that lay outside had a feel of magic –
the magic of a brand-new world as yet unsullied by the
hand and tools of men, a clean place that had no litter in
it. If he went out and walked in it, he wondered, would
the presence of himself, a human who had no right to be
there, subtract something from the magic?

Out in the hall, he took the elevator to the ground
floor. Just off the corridor lay the lounge and the outer
door opened from the lounge. Walking softly, although
he could not explain why he went so softly, for in this
sleeping place there was no one to disturb, he went into
the lounge.

As he reached the door, he heard voices and, halting in
the shadow, glanced rapidly over the room to locate the
speakers. There were three of them sitting at a table in
the far end of the loung. Bottles and glasses stood upon
the table, but they did not seem to be drinking; they were
hunched forward, heads close together, engaged in
earnest conversation.

As he watched, one of them reared back in his chair,
speaking in anger, his voice rising. 'I warned you,' he
shouted. 'I warned Breen and I warned you, Gale. And
you laughed at me.'

It was Sutton who was speaking. The man was too
distant and the light too dim for Latimer to recognize his
features, but the voice he was sure of.

'I did not laugh at you,' protested Gale.

'Perhaps not you, but Breen did.'

'I don't know about Breen or laughter,' said the third
man, 'but there's been too much going wrong. Not just

the three suicides. Other things as well. Miscalculations, erroneous data processing, bad judgments. Things all screwed up. Take the generator failure the other day. Three hours that we were without power, the fence without power. You know what that could mean if several big carnivores . . .'

'Yes, we know,' said Gale, 'but that was a mere technical malfunction. Those things happen. The one that worries me is this fellow, Latimer. That was a pure and simple foul-up. There was no reason to put him into Auk House. It cost a hell of a lot of money to do so; a very tricky operation. And when he got there, what happens? He escapes. I tell you, gentlemen, there are too many foul-ups. More than can be accounted for in the normal course of operation.'

'There is no use trying to cover it up, to make a mystery out of it,' said Sutton. 'You know and I know what is happening, and the sooner we admit we know and start trying to figure out what to do about it, the better it will be. If there is anything we can do about it. We're up against an intelligence that may be as intelligent as we are, but in a different way. In a way that we can't fight. Mental power against technical power, and in a case like that, I'd bet on mental power. I warned you months ago. Treat these jokers with kid gloves, I told you. Do nothing to upset them. Handle them with deference. Think kindly toward them, because maybe they can tell what you're thinking. I believe they can. And then what happens? A bunch of lunkheads go out for an afternoon of shooting and when they find no other game, use these friends of ours for casual target practice . . .'

'But that was months ago,' said the third man.

'They're testing,' said Sutton. 'Finding out what they can do. How far they can go. They can stop a generator. They can mess up evaluations. They can force men to kill themselves. God knows what else they can do. Give them a few more weeks. And, by the way, what particular brand of idiocy persuaded prime world to site the base of operations in a world like this?'

'There were many considerations,' said Gale. 'For one thing, it seemed a safe place. If some opposition should try to move in on us . . .'

'You're insane,' shouted Sutton. 'There isn't any opposition. How could there be opposition?'

Moving swiftly, Latimer crossed the corner of the lounge, eased his way out of the door. Looking back over his shoulder, he saw the three still sitting at the table. Sutton was shoutng, banging his fist on the table-top.

Gale was shrilling at him, his voice rising over Sutton's shoutng: 'How the hell could we suspect there was intelligence here? A world of stupid lizards . . .'

Latimer stumbled across the stone-paved terrace and went down the short flight of stone stairs that took him to the lawn. The world still was silver magic, a full moon riding in a cloudless sky. There was a softness in the air, a cleanness in the air.

But he scarcely noticed the magic and the cleanness. One thing thundered in his brain. A mistake! He should not have been sent to Auk House. There had been a miscalculation. Because of the mental machination of a reptilian intelligence on this world where the Cretaceous had not ended, he had been snatched from prime world. Although the fault, he realized, did not lie in this world, but in prime world itself – in the scheme that had been hatched to make prime world and the alternate worlds safe, safe beyond all question, for prime world's business interests.

He walked out across the sward and looked up at the northern hilltop. A row of huddled figures sat there, a long row of dumpy reptilian figures solemnly staring down at the invaders who had dared to desecrate their world.

He had wondered, Latimer remembered, how one man alone might manage to put an end to the prime-world project, knowing well enough that no one man could do it, perhaps that no conceivable combination of men could do it.

But now he need wonder no longer. In time to come, sooner or later, an end would come to it. Maybe by that time, most of the personnel here would have have been transferred to Auk House or to other stations, fleeing this doomed place. It might be that in years to come, another operations center would be set up on some safer world and the project would go on. But at least some time would be bought for the human race; perhaps the project might be dropped. It already had cost untold billions. How much more would the prime-world managers be willing to put into it? That was the crux of it, he knew, the crux of everything on prime world: was it worth the cost?

He turned about to face the hilltop squarely and those who squatted there. Solemnly, David Latimer, standing in the magic moonlight, raised an arm in salutation to them.

He knew even as he did it that it was a useless gesture, a gesture for himself rather than for those dumpy figures sitting on the hilltop, who would neither see nor know. But even so, it was important that he do it, important that he, an intelligent human, pay a measure of sincere respect to an intelligence of another species in recognition of his belief that a common code of ethics might be shared.

The figures on the hilltop did not stir. Which, he told himself, was no more than he had expected of them. How should they know, why should they care what he instinctively had tried to communicate to them, not really expecting to communicate, but at least to make some sign, if to no other than himself, of the sense of fellowship that he, in that moment, felt for them?

As he was thinking this, he felt a warmness come upon

him, encompassing him, enfolding him, as when he had been a child, in dim memory, he remembered his mother tucking him snugly into bed. Then he was moving, being lifted and impelled, with the high guard fence below him and the face of the great hill sliding underneath him. He felt no fright, for he seemed to be in a dreamlike state inducing a belief, deep-seated, that what was happening was not happening and that, in consequence, no harm could come to him.

He faced the dark and huddled figures, all sitting in a row, and although he still was dream-confused, he could see them clearly. They were nothing much to look at. They were as dumpy and misshapen as they had seemed when he had seen them from a distance. Their bodies were graceless lumps, the details vague even in the bright moonlight, but the faces he never would forget. They had the sharp triangle of the reptilian skull, the cruelty of the sharpness softened by the liquid compassion of the eyes.

Looking at them, he wondered if he was really there, if he was facing them, as he seemed to be, or if he still might be standing on the greensward of the compound, staring up the hill at the huddled shapes, which now seemed to be only a few feet distant from him. He tried to feel the ground beneath his feet, to press his feet against the ground, a conscious effort to orient himself, and, try as he might, he could feel no ground beneath his feet.

They were not awesome creatures and there was nothing horrible about them – just a faint distastefulness. They squatted in their limpy row and stared at him out of the soft liquid of their eyes. And he felt – in some strange way that he could not recognize, he felt the presence of them. Not as if they were reaching out physically to touch him – fearing that if they did touch him, he would recoil from them – but in another kind of reaching, as if they were pouring into him, as one might pour water in a bottle, an essence of themselves.

Then they spoke to him, not with voice, not with words, with nothing at all that he could recognize – perhaps, he thought wildly, they spoke with that essence of themselves they were pouring into him.

'Now that we have met,' they said, 'we'll send you back again.'

And he was back.

He stood at the end of the brick-paved driveway that led up to the house, and behind him he heard the damp and windy rustle of a primeval forest, with two owls chuckling throatily in the trees behind him. A few windows in the house were lighted. Great oaks grew upon the spreading lawn, and beneath the trees stood graceful stone benches that had the look of never being used.

Auk House, he told himself. They had sent him back to Auk House, not back to the grassy compound that lay inside the fence in that other world where the Cretaceous had not ended.

Inside himself he felt the yeasty churning of the essence that the squatting row of monstrosities had poured into him, and out of it he gained a knowledge and a comfort.

Policemen, he wondered, or referees, perhaps? Creatures that would monitor the efforts of those entre-preneurs who sought a monopoly of all the alternate worlds that had been opened for humans, and perhaps for many other races. They would monitor and correct, making certain that the worlds would not fall prey to the multinational financial concepts of the race that had opened them, but would become the heritage and birth-right of those few intelligent peoples that had risen on this great multiplicity of worlds, seeing to it that the worlds would be used in a wiser context than prime world had been used by humans.

Never doubting for a moment that it would or could be

done, knowing for a certainty that it would come about, that in the years to come men and other intelligences would live on the paradise worlds that Sutton had told him of – and all the other worlds that lay waiting to be used with an understanding the human race had missed. Always with those strange, dumpy ethical wardens who would sit on many hilltops to keep their vigil.

Could they be trusted? he wondered, and was ashamed of thinking it. They had looked into his eyes and had poured their essence into him and had returnd him here, not back to the Cretaceous compound. They had known where it was best for him to go and they would know all the rest of it.

He started up the driveway, his heels clicking on the bricks. As he came up to the stoop the door came open and the man in livery stood there.

'You're a little late,' said the butler. 'The others waited for you, but just now sat down to dinner. I'm sure the soup's still warm.'

'I'm sorry,' said Latimer. 'I was unavoidably de-tained.'

'Some of the others thought they should go out looking for you, but Mr Jonathon dissuaded them. He said you'd be all right. He said you had your wits about you. He said you would be back.'

The butler closed the door behind him. 'They'll all be very happy to find you're back,' he said.

'Thank you,' said Latimer.

He walked, trying not to hurry, fighting down the happiness he felt welling up inside himself, toward the doorway from which came the sound of bright laughter and sprightly conversation.

Kindergarten

He went walking in the morning before the Sun was up, down past the old, dilapidated barn that was falling in upon itself, across the stream and up the slope of pasture ankle-deep with grass and summer flowers, when the world was wet with dew and the chill edge of night still lingered in the air.

He went walking in the morning because he knew he might not have too many mornings left; any day, the pain might close down for good and he was ready for it – he'd been ready for it for a long time now.

He was in no hurry. He took each walk as if it were his last and he did not want to miss a single thing on any of the walks – the turned-up faces of the pasture roses with the tears of dew running down their cheeks or the matins of the birds in the thickets that ran along the ditches.

He found the machine alongside the path that ran through a thicket at the head of a ravine. At first glance, he was irritated by it, for it was not only unfamiliar, but an incongruous thing as well, and he had no room in heart or mind for anything but the commonplace. It had been the commonplace, the expected, the basic reality of Earth and the life one lived on it which he had sought in coming to this abandoned farm, seeking out a place where he might stand on ground of his own choosing to meet the final day.

He stopped in the path and stood there, looking at this

strange machine, feeling the roses and the dew and the
early morning bird song slip away from him, leaving him
alone with this thing beside the path which looked for all
the world like some fugitive from a home appliance shop.
But as he looked at it, he began to see the little
differences and he knew that here was nothing he'd ever
seen before or heard of – that it most certainly was not a
wandering automatic washer or a delinquent de-
humidifier.

For one thing, it shone – not with surface metallic
lustre or the gleam of sprayed-on porcelain, but with a
shine that was all the way through whatever it was made
of. If you looked at it just right, you got the impression
that you were seeing into it, though not clearly enough to
be able to make out the shape of any of its innards. It was
rectangular, at a rough guess three feet by four by two,
and it was without knobs for one to turn or switches to
snap on or dials to set – which suggested that it was not
something one was meant to operate.

He walked over to it and bent down and ran his hand
along its top, without thinking why he should reach out
and touch it, knowing when it was too late that probably
he should have left it alone. But it seemed to be all right
to touch it, for nothing happened – not right away, at
least. The metal, or whatever it was made of, was smooth
to the hand and beneath the sleekness of its surface he
seemed to sense a terrible hardness and a frightening
strength.

He took his hand away and straightened up, stepped
back.

The machine clicked, just once, and he had the dis-
tinct impression that it clicked not because it had to click
to operate, not because it was turning itself on, but to
attract attention, to let him know that it was an
operating machine and that it had a function and was
ready to perform it. And he got the impression that for

whatever purpose it might operate, it would do so with high efficiency and a minimum of noise.

Then it laid an egg.

Why he thought of it in just that way, he never was able to explain, even later when he had thought about it.

But, anyhow, it laid an egg, and the egg was a piece of jade, green with milky whiteness running through it, and exquisitely carved with what appeared to be *outré* symbolism.

He stood there in the path, looking at the jade, for a moment forgetting in his excitement how it had materialized, caught up by the beauty of the jade itself and the superb workmanship that had wrought it into shape. It was, he told himself, the finest piece that he had ever seen and he knew exactly how its texture would feel beneath his fingers and just how expertly, upon close examination, he would find the carving had been done.

He bent and picked it up and held it lovingly between his hands, comparing it with the pieces he had known and handled for years in the museum. But now, even with the jade between his hands, the museum was a misty place, far back along the corridors of time, although it had been less than three months since he had walked away from it.

'Thank you,' he said to the machine and an instant later thought what a silly thing to do, talking to a machine as if it were a person.

The machine just sat there. It did not click again and it did not move.

So finally he left, walking back to the old farmhouse on the slope above the barn.

In the kitchen, he placed the jade in the centre of the table, where he could see it while he worked. He kindled a fire in the stove and fed in split sticks of wood, not too large, to make quick heat. He put the kettle on to warm and got dishes from the pantry and set his place. He fried bacon and drained it on paper towelling and cracked the last of the eggs into the skillet.

He ate, staring at the jade that stood in front of him, admiring once again its texture, trying to puzzle out the symbolism of its carving and finally wondering what it might be worth. Plenty, he thought – although, of all considerations, that was the least important.

The carving puzzled him. It was in no tradition that he had ever seen or of which he had ever read. What it was meant to represent, he could not imagine. And yet it had a beauty and a force, a certain character, that tagged it as no haphazard doodling, but as the product of a highly developed culture.

He did not hear the young woman come up the steps and walk across the porch, but first knew that she was there when she rapped upon the door frame. He looked up from the jade and saw her standing in the open kitchen doorway and at first sight of her he found himself, ridiculously, thinking of her in the same terms he had been thinking of the jade.

The jade was cool and green and she was crisp and white, but her eyes, he thought, had the soft look of this wondrous piece of jade about them, except that they were blue.

'Hello, Mr Chaye,' she said.

'Good morning,' he replied.

She was Mary Mallet, Johnny's sister.

'Johnny wanted to go fishing,' Mary told him. 'He and the little Smith boy. So I brought the milk and eggs.'

'I am pleased you did,' said Peter, 'although you should not have bothered. I could have walked over later. It would have done me good.'

He immediately regretted that last sentence, for it was something he was thinking too much lately – that such and such an act or the refraining from an act would do him good when, as a matter of plain fact, there was nothing that would help him at all. The doctors had made at least that much clear to him.

He took the eggs and milk and asked her in and went to place the milk in the cooler, for he had no electricity for a refrigerator.

'Have you had breakfast?' he asked.

Mary said she had.

'It's just as well,' he said wryly. 'My cooking's pretty bad. I'm just camping out, you know.'

And regretted that one, too.

Chaye, he told himself, quit being so damn maudlin.

'What a pretty thing!' exclaimed Mary. 'Wherever did you get it?'

'The jade? Now, that's a funny thing. I found it.'

She reached a hand out for it.

'May I?'

'Certainly,' said Peter.

He watched her face as she picked it up and held it in both hands, carefully, as he had held it.

'You *found* this?'

'Well, I didn't exactly find it, Mary. It was given to me.'

'A friend?'

'I don't know.'

'That's a funny thing to say.'

'Not so funny. I'd like to show you the – well, the character who gave it to me. Have you got a minute?'

'Of course I have,' said Mary, 'although I'll have to hurry. Mother's canning peaches.'

They went down the slope together, past the barn, and crossed the creek to come into the pasture. As they walked up the pasture, he wondered if they would find it there, if it still was there – or ever had been there.

It was.

'What an outlandish thing!' said Mary.

'That's the word exactly,' Peter agreed.

'What is it, Mr Chaye?'

'I don't know.'

'You said you were given the jade. You don't mean . . .'

'But I do,' said Peter.

They moved closer to the machine and stood watching it. Peter noticed once again the shine of it and the queer sensation of being able to see into it – not very far, just part way, and not very well at that. But still the metal or whatever it was could be seen into, and that was somehow uncomfortable.

Mary bent over and ran her fingers along its top.

'It feels all right,' she said. 'Just like porcelain or—'

The machine clicked and a flacon lay upon the grass.

'For you,' said Peter.

'For me?'

Peter picked up the tiny bottle and handed it to her. It was a triumph of glassblower's skill and it shone with sparkling prismatic colour in the summer sunlight.

'Perfume would be my guess,' he said.

She worked the stopper loose.

'Lovely,' she breathed and held it out to him to smell.

It was all of lovely.

She corked it up again.

'But, Mr Chaye . . .'

'I don't know,' said Peter. 'I simply do not know.'

'Not even a guess?'

He shook his head.

'You just found it here.'

'I was out for a walk—'

'And it was waiting for you.'

'Well, now . . .' Peter began to object, but now that he thought about it, that seemed exactly right – he had not found the machine; it had been waiting for him.

'It was, wasn't it?'

'Now that you mention it,' said Peter, 'yes, I guess it was waiting for me.'

Not for him specifically, perhaps, but for anyone who might come along the path. It had been waiting to be found, waiting for a chance to go into its act, to do whatever it was supposed to do.

For now it appeared, as plain as day, that someone had left it there.

He stood in the pasture with Mary Mallet, farmer's daughter, standing by his side – with the familiar grasses and the undergrowth and trees, with the shrill of locust screeching across the rising heat of day, with the far-off tinkle of a cowbell – and felt the chill of the thought within his brain, the cold and terrible thought backgrounded by the black of space and the dim end-lessness of time. And he felt, as well, a *reaching* out of something, of a chilly alien thing, towards the warmth of humanity and Earth.

'Let's go back,' he said.

They returned across the pasture to the house and stood for a moment at the gate.

'Isn't there something we should do?' asked Mary. 'Someone we should tell about it?'

He shook his head. 'I want to think about it first.'

'And do something about it?'

'There may be nothing that anyone can or should do.'

He watched her go walking down the road, then turned away and went back to the house.

He got out the lawn mower and cut the grass. After the lawn was mowed, he pottered in the flower-bed. The zinnias were coming along fine, but something had got into the asters and they weren't doing well. And the grass kept creeping in, he thought. No matter what he did, the grass kept creeping into the bed to strangle out the plants.

After lunch, he thought, maybe I'll go fishing. Maybe going fishing will do me—

He caught the thought before he finished it.

He squatted by the flower-bed, dabbing at the ground with the point of his gardening trowel, and thought about the machine out in the pasture.

I want to think about it, he'd told Mary, but what was there to think about? Something that someone had left in his pasture – a machine that clicked and laid a gift like an egg when you patted it.

What did that mean?

Why was it here?

Why did it click and hand out a gift when you patted it?

Response? The way a dog would wag its tail?

Gratitude? For being noticed by a human?

Negotiation?

Friendly gesture?

Booby trap?

And how had it known he would have sold his soul for a piece of jade one-half as fine as the piece it had given him?

How had it known a girl would like perfume?

He heard the running footsteps behind him and swung around and there was Mary, running across the lawn.

She reached him and went down on her knees beside him and her hands clutched his arm.

'Johnny found it, too,' she panted. 'I ran all the way. Johnny and that Smith boy found it. They cut across the pasture coming home from fishing . . .'

'Maybe we should have reported it,' said Peter.

'It gave them something, too. A rod and reel to Johnny and a baseball bat and mitt to little Augie Smith.'

'Oh, good Lord!'

'And now they're telling everyone.'

'It doesn't matter,' Peter said. 'At least, I don't suppose it matters.'

'What is that thing out there? You said you didn't know. But you have some idea. Peter, you must have some idea.'

'I think it's alien,' Peter reluctantly and embarrassedly told her. 'It has a funny look about it, like nothing I've ever seen or read about, and Earth machines don't give away things when you lay a hand on them. You have to feed them coins first. This isn't – isn't from Earth.'

'From Mars, you mean?'

'Not from Mars,' said Peter. 'Not from this solar system. We have no reason to think another race of high intelligence exists in this solar system and whoever dreamed up that machine had plenty of intelligence.'

'But . . . not from this solar system . . .'

'From some other star.'

'The stars are so far away!' she protested.

So far away, thought Peter. So far out of the reach of the human race. Within the reach of dreams, but not the reach of hands. So far away and so callous and uncaring. And the machine—

'Like a slot machine,' he said, 'except it always pays in jackpots and you don't even need a coin. That is crazy, Mary. That's one reason it isn't of this Earth. No Earth machine, no Earth inventor, would do that.'

'The neighbours will be coming,' Mary said.

'I know they will. They'll be coming for their hand-outs.'

'But it isn't very big. It could not carry enough inside it for the entire neighbourhood. It does not have much more than room enough for the gifts it's already handed out.'

'Mary, did Johnny want a rod and reel?'

'He'd talked of practically nothing else.'

'And you like perfume?'

'I'd never had any good perfume. Just cheap stuff.' She laughed nervously. 'And you? Do you like jade?'

'I'm what you might call a minor expert on it. It's a passion with me.'

'Then that machine . . .'

'Gives each one the thing he wants,' Peter finished for her.

'It's frightening,' said Mary.

And it seemed strange that anything at all could be frightening on such a day as this – a burnished summer day, with white clouds rimming the western horizon and the sky the colour of pale blue silk, a day that had no moods, but was as commonplace as the cornfield earth.

After Mary had left, Peter went in the house and made his lunch. He sat by the window, eating it, and watched the neighbours come. They came by twos and threes, tramping across the pasture from all directions, coming to his pasture from their own farms, leaving the haying rigs and the cultivators, abandoning their work in the middle of the day to see the strange machine. They stood around and talked, tramping down the thicket where he had found the machine, and at times their high, shrill voices drifted across to him, but he could not make out what they said, for the words were flattened and distorted by the distance.

From the stars, he'd said. From some place among the stars.

And if that be fantasy, he said, I have a right to it.

First contact, he thought. And clever!

Let an alien being arrive on Earth and the women would run screaming for their homes and the men would grab their rifles and there'd be hell to pay.

But a machine – that was a different matter. What if it was a little different? What if it acted a little strangely? After all, it was only a machine. It was something that could be understood.

And if it handed out free gifts, that was all the better.

After lunch, he went out and sat on the steps and some of the neighbours came and showed him what the machine had given them. They sat around and talked, all of them excited and mystified, but not a single one of them was scared.

Among the gifts were wrist-watches and floor lamps,

typewriters and fruit juicers, sets of dishes, chests of silver, bolts of drapery materials, shoes, shotguns, carving sets, book ends, neckties, and many other items. One youngster had a dozen skunk traps and another had a bicycle.

A modern Pandora's box, thought Peter, made by an alien intelligence and set down upon the Earth.

Apparently the word was spreading, for now the people came in cars. Some of them parked by the road and walked down to the pasture and others came into the barnyard and parked there, not bothering to ask for permission.

After a time, they would come back loaded with their loot and drive away. Out in the pasture was a milling throng of people. Peter, watching it, was reminded of a county fair or a village carnival.

By chore-time, the last of them had gone, even the neighbours who had come to say a few words with him and to show him what they'd gotten, so he left the house and walked up the pasture slope.

The machine still was there and it was starting to build something. It had laid out around it a sort of platform of a stone that looked like marble, as if it were laying a foundation for a building. The foundation was about ten feet by twelve and was set level against the pasture's slope, with footings of the same sort of stone going down into the ground.

He sat down on a stump a little distance away and looked out over the peace of the countryside. It seemed more beautiful, more quiet and peaceful than it had ever seemed before, and he sat there contentedly, letting the evening soak into his soul.

The sun had set not more than half an hour ago. The western sky was a delicate lemon fading into green, with here and there the pink of wandering clouds, while beneath the horizon the land lay in the haze of a blue twilight, deepening at the edges. The liquid evensong of birds ran along the hedges and the thickets and the whisper of swallows' wings came down from overhead.

This is Earth, he thought, the peaceful, human Earth, a lanscape shaped by an agricultural people. This is the Earth of plum blossom and of proud red barns and of corn rows as straight as rifle barrels.

For millions of years, the Earth had lain thus, without interference; a land of soil and life, a local corner of the Galaxy engaged in its own small strivings.

And now?

Now, finally, there was interference.

Now, finally, someone or something had come into this local corner of the Galaxy and Earth was alone no longer.

To himself, he knew, it did not matter. Physically, there was no longer anything that possibly could matter to him. All that was left was the morning brightness and the evening peace and from each of these, from every hour of each day that was left to him, it was his purpose to extract the last bit of joy in being alive.

But to the others it would matter – to Mary Mallet and her brother Johnny, to the little Smith boy who had got the baseball bat and mitt, to all the people who had visited this pasture, and to all the millions who had not visited or even heard of it.

Here, in this lonely place in the midst of the great cornlands, had come, undramatically, a greater drama than the Earth had yet known. Here was the pivot point.

He said to the machine: 'What do you intend with us?'

There was no answer.

He had not expected one.

He sat and watched the shadows deepen and the lights spring up in the farm houses that were sprinkled on the land. Dogs barked from far away and others answered them and the cowbells rang across the hills like tiny vesper notes.

At last, when he could see no longer, he walked slowly back to the house.

In the kitchen, he found a lamp and lit it. He saw by the kitchen clock that it was almost nine o'clock – time for the evening news.

He went into the living-room and turned on the radio. Sitting in the dark, he listened to it.

There was good news.

There had been no polio deaths in the state that day and only one new case had been reported.

'It is too soon to hope, of course,' the newscaster said, 'but it definitely is the first break in the epidemic. Up to the time of broadcast, there have been no new cases for more than twenty hours. The state health director said . . .'

He went on to read what the health director said, which wasn't much of anything, just one of those public statements which pretty generally add up to nothing tangible.

It was the first day in almost three weeks, the newscaster had said, during which no polio deaths had been reported. But despite the development, he said, there still was need of nurses. If you are a nurse, he added, won't you please call this number? You are badly needed.

He went on to warm over a grand jury report, without adding anything really new. He gave the weather broadcast. He said the Emmett murder trial had been postponed another month.

Then he said: 'Someone has just handed me a bulletin. Now let me see . . .'

You could hear the paper rustling as he held it to read it through, could hear him gasp a little.

'It says here,' he said, 'that Sheriff Joe Burns has just now been notified that a Flying Saucer has landed on the Peter Chaye farm out near Mallet Corners. No one seems to know too much about it. One report is that it was found this morning, but no one thought to notify the sheriff. Let me repeat – this is just a report. We don't know any more than what we've told you. We don't know if it is true or not. The sheriff is on his way there now. We'll let you know as soon as we learn anything. Keep tuned to this . . .'

Peter got up and turned off the radio. Then he went into the kitchen to bring in the lamp. He set the lamp on a table and sat down again to wait for Sheriff Burns.

He didn't have long to wait.

'Folks tell me,' said the sheriff, 'this here Flying Saucer landed on your farm.'

'I don't know if it's a Flying Saucer, Sheriff.'

'Well, what is it, then?'

'I wouldn't know,' said Peter.

'Folks tell me it was giving away things,' the Sheriff said wryly.

'It was doing that, all right.'

'If this is some cockeyed advertising stunt,' the sheriff said, 'I'll have someone's neck for it.'

'I'm sure it's not an advertising stunt.'

'Why didn't you notify me right off? What you mean by holding out on a thing like this?'

'I didn't think of notifying you,' Peter told him. 'I wasn't trying to hold out on anything.'

'You new around here, ain't you?' asked the sheriff. 'I don't recollect seeing you before. Thought I knew everyone.'

'I've been here three months.'

'Folks tell me you ain't farming the place. Tell me you ain't got no family. Live here all by yourself, just doing nothing.'

'That's correct,' said Peter.

The sheriff waited for the explanation, but Peter offered none. The sheriff looked at him suspiciously in the smoky lamplight.

'Can you show us this here Flying Saucer?'

By now Peter was a little weary of the sheriff, so he said, 'I can tell you how to find it. You go down past the barn and cross the brook . . .'

'Why don't you come with us, Chaye?'

'Look, Sheriff, I was telling you how to find it. Do you want me to continue?'

'Why, sure,' the sheriff said. 'Of course I do. But why can't you . . .'

'I've seen it twice,' said Peter. 'I've been overrun by people all the afternoon.'

'All right, all right,' the sheriff said. 'Tell me how to find it.'

He told him and the sheriff left, followed by his two deputies.

The telephone rang.

Peter answered it. It was the radio station he'd been listening to.

'Say,' asked the radio reporter, 'you got a Saucer out there?'

'I don't think so,' Peter said. 'I do have something out here, though. The sheriff is going to take a look at it.'

'We want to send out our mobile TV unit, but we wanted to be sure there was something there. It be all right with you if we send it out?'

'No objections. Send it along.'

'You sure you got something there?'

'I told you that I had.'

'Well, then suppose you tell me . . .'

Fifteen minutes later, he hung up.

The phone rang again.

It was the Associated Press. The man at the other end of the wire was wary and sceptical.

'What's this I hear about a Saucer out there?'

Ten minutes later, Peter hung up.

The phone rang almost immediately.

'McClelland of the *Tribune*,' said a bored voice. 'I heard a screwball story . . .'

Five minutes.

The phone rang again.

It was the United Press.

'Hear you got a Saucer. Any little men in it?'

Fifteen minutes.

The phone rang.

It was an irate citizen.

'I just heard on the radio you got a Flying Saucer. What kind of gag you trying to pull? You know there ain't any Flying Saucers . . .'

'Just a moment, sir,' said Peter.

He let the receiver hang by its cord and went out to the kitchen. He found a pair of clips and came back. He could hear the irate citizen still chewing him out, the voice coming ghostlike out of the dangling receiver.

He went outside and found the wire and clipped it. When he came back in again, the receiver was silent. He hung it carefully on the hook.

Then he locked the doors and went to bed.

To bed, but not immediately to sleep. He lay beneath the covers, staring up into the darkness and trying to quiet the turmoil of speculation that surged within his brain.

He had gone walking in the morning and found a machine. He had put his hand upon it and it had given him a gift. Later on, it had given other gifts.

'A machine came, bearing gifts,' he said into the darkness.

A clever, calculated, well-worked-out first contact.

Contact them with something they will know and recognize and need not be afraid of, something to which they can feel superior.

Make it friendly – and what is more friendly than handing out a gift?

What is it?

Missionary?

Trader?

Diplomat?

Or just a mere machine and nothing more?

Spy? Adventurer? Investigator? Surveyor?

Doctor? Lawyer? Indian chief?

And why, of all places, had it landed here, in this forsaken farmland, in his pasture on his farm?

And its purpose?

What had been the purpose, the almost inevitable motive, of those fictional alien beings who, in tales of fantasy, had landed on Earth?

To take over, of course. If not by force, then by infiltration or by friendly persuasion and compulsion; to take over not only Earth, but the human race as well.

The man from the radio station had been excited, the Associated Press man had been indignant that anyone should so insult his intelligence, the *Tribune* man had been bored and the United Press man flippant. But the citizen had been angry. He was being taken in by another Flying Saucer story and it was just too much.

The citizen was angry because he didn't want his little world disturbed. He wanted no interference. He had trouble enough of his own without things being messed up by a Saucer's landing. He had problems of his own – earning a living, getting along with his neighbours, planning his work, worrying about the polio epidemic.

Although the newscaster had said the polio situation seemed a little brighter – no new cases and no deaths. And that was a fine thing, for polio was pain and death and a terror on the land.

Pain, he thought.

I've had no pain to-day.

For the first time in many days, there has been no pain.

He lay stiff and still beneath the covers, examining

himself for pain. He knew just where it lurked, the exact spot in his anatomy where it lurked hidden out of sight. He lay and waited for it, fearful, now that he had thought of it, that he would find it there.

But it was not there.

He lay and waited for it, afraid that the very thought of it would conjure it up from its hiding-place. It did not come. He dared it to come, he invited it to show itself, he hurled mental jibes at it to lure it out. It refused to be lured.

He relaxed and knew that for the moment he was safe. But safe only temporarily, for the pain was still there. It bided its time, waited for its moment, would come when the time was right.

With careless abandon, trying to wipe out the future and its threat, he luxuriated in life without the pain. He listened to the house – the slightly settling joists that made the floor-boards creak, the thrum of the light summer wind against the weathered siding, the scraping of the elm branch against the kitchen roof.

Another sound. A knocking at the door. 'Chaye! Chaye, where are you?'

'Coming,' he called.

He found slippers and went to the door. It was the sheriff and his men.

'Light the lamp,' the sheriff said.

'You got a match?' Peter asked.

'Yeah, here are some.'

Groping in the dark, Peter found the sheriff's hand and the book of matches.

He located the table, slid his hand across the top and felt the lamp. He lit it and looked at the sheriff from across the table.

'Chaye,' the sheriff said, 'that thing is building something.'

'I know it is.'

'What's the gag?'

'There's no gag.'

'It gave me this,' the sheriff said.

He threw the object on the table.

'A gun,' said Peter.

'You ever see one like it?'

It was a gun, all right, about the size of a .45. But it had no trigger and the muzzle flared and the whole thing was made of some white, translucent substance.

Peter picked it up and found it weighed no more than half a pound or so.

'No,' said Peter. 'No, I've never seen one like it.' He put it back on the table, gingerly. 'Does it work?'

'It does,' the sheriff said. 'I tried it on your barn.'

'There ain't no barn no more,' said one of the deputies.

'No report, no flash, no nothing,' the sheriff added.

'Just no barn,' repeated the deputy, obsessed with the idea.

A car drove into the yard.

'Go out and see who's there,' said the sheriff.

One of the deputies went out.

'I don't get it,' complained the sheriff. 'They said Flying Saucer, but I don't think it's any Saucer. A box is all it is.'

'It's a machine,' said Peter.

Feet stamped across the porch and men came through the door.

'Newspapermen,' said the deputy who had gone out to see.

'I ain't got no statement, boys,' the sheriff said.

One of them said to Peter: 'You Chaye?'

Peter nodded.

'I'm Hoskins from the *Tribune*. This is Johnson from the AP. That guy over there with the sappy look is a photographer, name of Langly. Disregard him.'

He pounded Peter on the back. 'How does it feel to be

sitting in the middle of the century's biggest news break? Great stuff, hey, boy?'

Langly said: 'Hold it.'

A flash bulb popped.

'I got to use the phone', said Johnson. 'Where is it?'

'Over there,' said Peter. 'It's not working.'

'How come at a time like this?'

'I cut the wire.'

'Cut the wire! You crazy, Chaye?'

'There were too many people calling.'

'Now,' said Hoskins, 'wasn't that a hell of a thing to do?'

'I'll fix her up,' Langly offered. 'Anyone got a pair of pliers?'

The sheriff said, 'You boys hold on a minute.'

'Hurry up and get into a pair of pants,' Hoskins said to Peter. 'We'll want your picture on the scene. Standing with your foot on it like the guy that's just killed an elephant.'

'You listen here,' the sheriff said.

'What is it, Sheriff?'

'This here's important. Get it straight. You guys can't go messing around with it.'

'Sure it's important,' said Hoskins. 'That is why we're here. Millions of people standing around with their tongues hanging out for news.'

'Here are some pliers,' someone remarked.

'Leave me at that phone,' said Langly.

'What are we horsing around for?' asked Hoskins. 'Let's go and see it.'

'I gotta make a call,' said Johnson.

'Look here, boys,' the sheriff insisted in confusion. 'Wait—'

'What's it like, Sheriff? Figure it's a Saucer? How big is it? Does it make a clicking noise or something? Hey, Langly, take the sheriff's picture.'

'Just a minute,' Langly shouted from outside. 'I'm fixing up this wire.'

More feet came across the porch. A head was thrust into the door.

'TV truck,' the head said. 'This the place? How do we get out to the thing?'

The phone rang.

Johnson answered it.

'It's for you, Sheriff.'

The sheriff lumbered across the room. They waited, listening.

'Sure, this is Sheriff Burns . . . Yeah, it's out there, all right . . . Sure, I know. I've seen it . . . No, of course, I don't know what it is . . . Yes, I understand . . . Yes, sir . . . Yes, sir. I'll see to it, sir.'

He hung up the receiver and turned around to face them.

'That was military intelligence,' he said. 'No one is going out there. No one's moving from this house. This place is restricted as of this minute.'

He looked from one to another of them ferociously.

'Them's orders,' he told them.

'Oh, hell, said Hoskins.

'I came all the way out here,' bawled the TV man. 'I'm not going to come out here and not . . .'

'It isn't me that's doing the ordering,' said the sheriff. 'It's Uncle Sam. You boys take things easy.'

Peter went into the kichen and poked up the fire and set on the kettle.

'The coffee's there,' he said to Langly. 'I'll put on some clothes.'

Slowly, the night wore on. Hoskins and Johnson phoned in the information they had jotted down on folded copy paper, their pencils stabbing cryptic signs as they talked to Peter and the sheriff. After some argument with the sheriff about letting him go, Langly left with his pictures. The sheriff paced up and down the room.

The radio blared. The phone banged constantly.

They drank coffee and smoked cigarettes, littering the floor with ground-out stubs. More newsmen pulled in, were duly warned by the sheriff, and settled down to wait.

Someone brought out a bottle and passed it around. Someone else tried to start a poker game, but nobody was interested.

Peter went out to get an armload of wood. The night was quiet, with stars.

He glanced towards the pasture, but there was nothing there to see. He tried to make out the empty place where the barn had disappeared. It was too dark to tell whether the barn was there or not.

Death watch or the last dark hour before the dawn – the brightest, most wonderful dawn that Man had ever seen in all his years of striving?

The machine was building something out there, building something in the night.

And what was it building?

Shrine?

Trading Post?

Mission House?

Embassy?

Fort?

There was no way of knowing, no way that one could tell.

Whatever it was building, it was the first known outpost ever built by an alien race on the planet Earth.

He went back into the house with the load of wood.

'They're sending troops,' the sheriff told him.

'Tramp, tramp, tramp,' said Hoskins, dead-pan, cigarette hanging negligently to his underlip.

'The radio just said so,' the sheriff said. 'They called out the guard.'

Hoskins and Johnson did some more tramp-tramping.

'You guys better not horse around with them soldier boys,' the sheriff warned. 'They'll shove a bayonet . . .'

Hoskins made a noise like a bugle blowing the charge. Johnson grabbed two spoons and beat out galloping hoofs.

'The cavalry!' shouted Hoskins. 'By God, boys, we're saved!'

Someone said wearily: 'Can't you guys be your age?'

They sat around, as the night wore on, drinking coffee and smoking. They didn't do much talking.

The radio station finally signed off. Someone fooled around, trying to get another station, but the batteries were too weak to pull in anything. He shut the radio off. It had been some time now since the phone had rung.

Dawn was still an hour away when the guardsmen arrived, not marching, nor riding horses, but in five canvas-covered trucks.

The captain came in for just a moment to find out where this goddam obscenity Saucer was. He was the fidgety type. He wouldn't even stay for a cup of coffee. He went out yelling orders at the drivers.

Inside the house, the others waited and heard the five trucks growl away.

Dawn came and a building stood in the pasture, and it was a bit confusing, for you could see that it was being built in a way that was highly unorthodox. Whoever or whatever was building it had started on the inside and was building outward, so that you saw the core of the building, as if it were a building that was being torn down and someone already had ripped off the entire exterior.

It covered half an acre and was five stories high. It gleamed pink in the first light of the morning, a beautiful misty pink that made you choke up a little, remembering the colour of the dress the little girl next door had worn for her seventh birthday party.

The guardsmen were ringed around it, the morning light spattering off their bayonets as they stood the guard.

Peter made breakfast – huge stacks of flapjacks, all the bacon he had left, every egg he could find, a gallon or two of oatmeal, more coffee.

'We'll send out and get some grub,' said Hoskins. 'We'll make this right with you.'

After breakfast, the sheriff and the deputies drove back to the county seat. Hoskins took up a collection and went to town to buy groceries. The other newsmen stayed on. The TV truck got squared off for some wide-angle distance shots.

The telephone started jangling again. The newsmen took turns answering it.

Peter walked down the road to the Mallet farm to get eggs and milk.

Mary ran out to the gate to meet him. 'The neighbours are getting scared,' she said.

'They weren't scared yesterday,' said Peter. 'They walked right up and got their gifts.'

'But this is different, Peter. This is getting out of hand. The building . . .'

And that was it, of course. The building.

No one had been frightened of an innocent-appearing machine because it was small and friendly. It shone so prettily and it clicked so nicely and it handed out gifts. It was something that could be superficially recognized and it had a purpose that was understandable if one didn't look too far.

But the building was big and might get bigger still and it was being erected inside out. And who in all the world had ever seen a structure built as fast as that one – five stories in one single night?

'How do they do it, Peter?' Mary asked in a hushed little voice.

'I don't know,' he said. 'Some principle that is entirely alien to us, some process that men have never even though of, a way of doing things, perhaps, that starts on an entirely different premise than the human way.'

'But it's just the kind of building that men themselves would build,' she objected. 'Not that kind of stone, perhaps – maybe there isn't any stone like that in the entire world – but in every other way there's nothing strange about it. It looks like a big high school or a department store.'

'My jade was jade,' said Peter, 'and your perfume was perfume and the rod and reel that Johnny got was a regular rod and reel.'

'That means they know about us. They know all there is to know. Peter, they've been watching us!'

'I have no doubt of it.'

He saw the terror in her eyes and reached out a hand to draw her close and she came into his arms and he held her tightly and thought, even as he did so, how strange that he should be the one to extend comfort and assurance.

'I'm foolish, Peter.'

'You're wonderful,' he assured her.

'I'm not really scared.'

'Of course you're not.' He wanted to say, 'I love you,' but he knew that those words he could never say. Although the pain, he thought – the pain had not come this morning.

'I'll get the milk and eggs,' said Mary.

'Give me all you can spare. I have quite a crowd to feed.'

Walking back, he thought about the neighbours being frightened now and wondered how long it would be before the world got frightened too – how long before artillery would be wheeling into line, how long before an atom bomb would fall.

He stopped on the rise of the hill above the house and for the first time noticed that the barn was gone. It had been sheared off as cleanly as if cut with a knife, with the stump of the foundation sliced away at an angle.

He wondered if the sheriff still had the gun and supposed he had. And he wondered what the sheriff would do with it and why it had been given him. For, of all the gifts that he had seen, it was the only one that was not familiar to Earth.

In the pasture that had been empty yesterday, that had been only trees and grass and old, grassed-over ditches, bordered by the wild plum thickets and the hazel brush and blackberry vine, rose the building. It seemed to him that it was bigger than when he had seen it less than an hour before.

Back at the house, the newspapermen were sitting in the yard, looking at the building.

One of them said to him, 'The brass arrived. They're waiting in there for you.'

'Intelligence?' asked Peter.

The newsman nodded. 'A chicken colonel and a major.'

They were waiting in the living-room. The colonel was a young man with grey hair. The major wore a moustache, very military.

The colonel introduced himself. 'I'm Colonel Whitman. This is Major Rockwell.'

Peter put down his eggs and milk and nodded acknowledgment.

'You found this machine,' said the colonel.

'That is right.'

'Tell us about it,' said the colonel, so Peter told them about it.

'This jade,' the colonel said. 'Could we have a look at it?'

Peter went to the kitchen and got the jade. They passed it from one to the other, examining it closely, turning it over and over in their hands, a bit suspicious of it, but admiring it, although Peter could see they knew nothing about jade.

Almost as if he might have known what was in Peter's mind, the colonel lifted his eyes from the jade and looked at him.

'You know jade,' the colonel said.

'Very well,' said Peter.

'You've worked with it before?'

'In a museum.'

'Tell me about yourself.'

Peter hesitated – then told about himself.

'But why are you here?' the colonel asked.

'Have you ever been in a hospital, Colonel? Have you ever thought what it would be like to die there?'

The colonel nodded. 'I can see your point. But here you'll have no—'

'I won't wait that long.'

'Yes, yes,' the colonel said. 'I see.'

'Colonel,' said the major. 'Look at this, sir, if you will. This symbolism is the same . . .'

The colonel snatched it from his hands and looked.

'The same as on the letterhead!' he shouted.

The colonel lifted his head and stared at Peter, as if it had been the first time he had seen him, as if he were surprised at seeing him.

There was, suddenly, a gun in the major's hand, pointing at Peter, its muzzle a cold and steady eye.

Peter tried to throw himself aside.

He was too late.

The major shot him down.

Peter fell for a million years through a wool-grey nothingness that screamed and he knew it must be a dream, an endless atavistic dream of falling, brought down through all the years from incredibly remote fore-bears who had dwelt in trees and had lived in fear of falling. He tried to pinch himself to awaken from the dream, but he couldn't do it, since he had no hands to pinch with, and, after a time, it became apparent that he had no body to pinch. He was a disembodied consciousness hurtling through a gulf which seemed to have no boundaries.

He fell for a million years through the void that seemed to scream at him. At first the screaming soaked into him and filled his soul, since he had no body, with a terrible agony that went on and on, never quite reaching the breaking point that would send him into the release of insanity. But he got used to it after a time and as soon as he did, the screaming stopped and he plunged down through space in a silence that was more dreadful than the screaming.

He fell for ever and for ever and then it seemed that for ever ended, for he was at rest and no longer falling.

He saw a face. It was a face from incredibly long ago, a face that he once had seen and had long forgotten, and he searched back along his memory to try to identify it.

He couldn't see it too clearly, for it seemed to keep bobbing around so he couldn't pin it down. He tried and tried and couldn't and he closed his eyes to shut the face away.

'Chaye,' a voice said. 'Peter Chaye.'

'Go away,' said Peter.

The voice went away.

He opened his eyes again and the face was there, clearer now and no longer bobbing.

It was the colonel's face.

He shut his eyes again, remembering the steady eye of the gun the major had held. He'd jumped aside, or tried to, and he had been too slow. Something had happened and he'd fallen for a million years and here he was, with the colonel looking at him.

He'd been shot. That was the answer, of course. The major had shot him and he was in a hospital. But where had he been hit? Arm? Both arms seemed to be all right. Leg? Both legs were all right, too. No pain. No bandages. No casts.

The colonel said: 'He came to for just a minute, Doc, and now he's off again.'

'He'll be all right,' said Doc. 'Just give him time. You gave him too big a charge, that's all. It'll take a little time.'

'We must talk to him.'

'You'll have to wait.'

There was silence for a moment.

Then: 'You're absolutely sure he's human?'

'We've gone over every inch of him,' said Doc. 'If he isn't human, he's too good an imitation for us ever to find out.'

'He told me he had cancer,' the colonel said. 'Claimed he was dying of cancer. Don't you see, if he wasn't human, if there was something wrong, he could always try to make it look . . .'

'He hasn't any cancer. Not a sign of it! No sign he ever had it. No sign he ever will.'

Even with his eyes shut, Peter felt that he was agape with disbelief and amazement. He forced his eyes to stay closed, afraid that this was a trick.

'That other doctor,' the colonel said, 'told Peter Chaye four months ago he had six more months to live. He told him . . .'

Doc said, 'Colonel, I won't even try to explain it. All I can tell you is that the man lying on that bed hasn't got cancer. He's as healthy a man as you would wish to find.'

'It isn't Peter Chaye, then,' the colonel stated in a dogged voice. 'It's something that took over Peter Chaye or duplicated Peter Chaye or . . .'

Doc said, 'Now, now, Colonel. Let's stick to what we know.'

'You're sure he's a man, Doc?'

'I'm sure he's a human being, if that is what you mean.'

'No little differences? Just one seemingly unimportant deviation from the human norm?'

'None,' Doc said, 'and even if there were, it wouldn't prove what you are after. There could be minor mutational difference in anyone. The human body doesn't always run according to a blue-print.'

'There were differences in all that stuff the machine gave away. Little differences that came to light only on close examination – but differences that spelled out a margin between human and alien manufacture.'

'All right, then, so there were differences. So those things were made by aliens. I still tell you this man is a human being.'

'It all ties in so neatly,' the colonel declared. 'Chaye goes out and buys this place – this old, abandoned farm. He's eccentric as hell by the standards of that neighbourhood. By the very fact of his eccentricity, he invites attention, which might be undesirable, but at the same time his eccentricity might be used to cover up and smooth over anything he did out of the ordinary. It would be just somebody like him who'd supposedly find a strange machine. It would be . . .'

'You're building up a case,' said Doc, 'without anything to go on. You asked for one little difference in him to base your cockeyed theory on – no offence, but that's how I, as a doctor, see it. Well, now let's have one little fact – fact, mind you, not guess – to support this idea of yours.'

'What was in that barn?' demanded the colonel. 'That's what I want to know. Did Chaye build that machine in there? Was that why it was destroyed?'

'The sheriff destroyed the barn,' the doctor said. 'Chaye had nothing to do with it.'

'But who gave the gun to the sheriff? Chaye's machine,

that's who. And it would be an easy matter of suggestion, mind control, hypnotism, whatever you want to call it . . .'

'Let's get back to facts. You used an anaesthetic gun on this man. You've held him prisoner. By your orders, he has been subjected to intensive examination, a clear invasion of his privacy. I hope to God he never brings you into court. He could throw the book at you.'

'I know,' the colonel admitted reluctantly. 'But we have to bust this thing. We must find out what it is. We have got to get that bomb back!'

'The bomb's what worries you.'

'Hanging up there,' the colonel said, sounding as if he'd shuddered. 'Just hanging up there!'

'I have to get along,' replied the doctor. 'Take it easy, Colonel.'

The doctor's footsteps went out through the door and down the corridor, fading away. The colonel paced up and down a while then sat down heavily in a chair.

Peter lay in bed, and one thought crashed through his brain, one thought again and again:

I'm going to live!

But he hadn't been.

He had been ready for the day when the pain finally became too great to bear.

He had picked his ground to spend his final days, to make his final stand.

And now he had been reprieved. Now, somehow, he had been given back his life.

He lay in the bed, fighting against excitement, against a growing tenseness, trying to maintain the pretence that he still was under the influence of whatever he'd been shot with.

An anaesthetic gun, the doctor had said. Something new, something he had never heard of. And yet somewhere there was a hint of it. Something, he re-

membered, about dentistry – a new technique that
dentists used to desensitize the gums, a fine stream of
anaesthetic sprayed against the gums. Something like
that, only hundreds or thousands of times stronger?

Shot and brought here and examined because of some
wild fantasy lurking in the mind of a G-2 colonel.

Fantasy? He wondered. Unwitting, unsuspecting,
could he have played a part? It was ridiculous, of
course. For he remembered nothing he had done or said
or even thought which gave him a clue to any part he
might have played in the machine's coming to the
Earth.

Could cancer be something other than disease? Some
uninvited guest, perhaps, that came and lived within a
human body? A clever alien guest who came from far
away, across the unguessed light-years?

And that, he knew, was fantasy to match the colonel's
fantasy, a malignant nightmare of distrust that dwelt
within the human mind, an instinctive defence
mechanism that conditioned the race to expect the
worst and to arm against it.

There was nothing feared so much as the unknown
factor, nothing which one must guard against so much
as the unexplained.

We have to bust this thing, the colonel had said. We
must find out what it is.

And, that, of course, was the terror of it – that they
had no way of knowing what it was.

He stirred at last, very deliberately, and the colonel
spoke.

'Peter Chaye,' he said.

'Yes, what is it, Colonel?'

'I have to talk to you.'

'All right, talk to me.'

He sat up in bed and saw that he was in a hospital
room. It had the stark, antiseptic quality, the tile floor,

the colourless walls, the utilitarian look – and the bed on which he lay was a hospital bed.

'How do you feel?' the colonel asked.

'Not so hot,' confessed Peter.'

'We were a little rough on you, but we couldn't take a chance. There was the letter, you see, and the slot machines and the stamp machines and all the other things and . . .'

'You said something about a letterhead.'

'What do you know about that, Chaye?'

'I don't know a thing.'

'It came to the President,' said the colonel. 'A month or so ago. And a similar one went to every other administrative head on the entire Earth.'

'Saying?'

'That's the hell of it. It was written in no language known anywhere on Earth. But there was one line – one line on all the letters – that you could read. It said: "By the time you have deciphered, you'll be ready to act logically." And that was all anybody could read – one line in the native language of every country that got a copy of the letter. The rest was in gibberish, for all we could make of it.'

'You haven't deciphered it?'

He could see the colonel sweating. 'Not even a single character, much less a word.'

Peter reached out a hand to the bedside table and lifted the carafe, tipped it above the glass. There was nothing in it.

The colonel heaved himself out of his chair. 'I'll get you a drink of water.'

He picked up the glass and opened the bathroom door.

'I'll let it run a while and get it cold,' he said.

But Peter scarcely heard him, for he was staring at the door. There was a bolt on it and if—

The water started running and the colonel raised his voice to be heard above it.

'That's about the time we started finding the machines,' he said. 'Can you imagine it? A cigarette-vending machine and you could buy cigarettes from it, but it was more than that. It was something watching you. Something that studied the people and the way they lived. And the stamp machines and the slot machines and all the other mechanical contrivances that we have set up. Not machines, but watchers. Watching all the time. Watching and learning . . .'

Peter swung his legs out of bed and touched the floor. He approached swiftly and silently on bare feet and slammed the door, then reached up and slid the bolt. It snicked neatly into place.

'Hey!' the colonel shouted.

Clothes?

They might be in the closet.

Peter leaped at it and wrenched the door open and there they were hung upon the hangers.

He ripped off the hospital gown, snatched at his trousers and pulled them on.

Shirt, now! In a drawer.

And shoes? There on the closet floor. Don't take time to tie them.

The colonel was pushing and hammering at the door, not yelling yet. Later he would, but right now he was intent on saving all the face he could. He wouldn't want to advertise immediately the fact that he'd been tricked.

Peter felt through his pockets. His wallet was gone. So was everything else – his knife, his watch, his keys. More than likely they'd taken all of it and put it in the office safe when he'd been brought in.

No time to worry about any of them. The thing now was to get away.

He went out of the door and down the corridor,

carefully not going too fast. He passed a nurse, but she scarcely glanced at him.

He found a stairway door and opened it. Now he could hurry just a little more. He went down the stairs three at a time, shoelaces clattering.

The stairs, he told himself, were fairly safe. Almost no one would use them when there were the elevators. He stopped and bent over for a moment and tied the laces.

The floor numbers were painted above each of the doors, so he knew where he was. At the ground floor, he entered the corridor again. So far, there seemed to be no alarms, although any minute now the colonel would start to raise a ruckus.

Would they try to stop him at the door? Would there be someone to question him? Would—

A basket of flowers stood beside a door. He glanced up and down the corridor. There were several people, but they weren't looking at him. He scooped up the flowers.

At the door, he said to the attendant who sat behind the desk: 'Mistake. Wrong flowers.'

She smiled sourly, but made no move to stop him.

Outside, he put the flowers down on the steps and walked rapidly away.

An hour later, he knew that he was safe. He knew also tha he was in a city thirty miles away from where he wanted to go and that he had no money and that he was hungry and his feet were sore from walking on the hard and unyielding concrete of the sidewalks.

He found a park and sat down on a bench. A little distance away, a group of old men were playing checkers at a table. A mother wheeled her baby. A young man sat on a nearby bench, listening to a tiny radio.

The radio said: '. . . apparently the building is completed. There has been no sign of it growing for the last eighteen hours. At the moment, it measures a thousand stories high and covers more than a hundred acres. The bomb, which was dropped two days ago, still floats there above it, held in suspension by some strange force. Artillery is standing by, waiting for the word to fire, but the word has not come through. Many think that since the bomb could not get through, shells will have no better chance, if any at all.

'A military spokesman, in fact, has said that the big guns are mere precautionary measures, which may be all right, but it certainly doesn't explain why the bomb was dropped. There is a rising clamour, not only in Congress, but throughout the world, to determine why an attempt was made at bombing. There has as yet been no hostile move directed from the building. The only damage so far reported has been the engulfment by the building of the farm home of Peter Chaye, the man who found the machine.

'All trace has been lost of Chaye since three days ago, when he suffered an attack of some sort and was taken from his home. It is believed that he may be in military custody. There is wide speculation on what Chaye may or may not know. It is entirely likely that he is the only man on Earth who can shed any light on what has happened on his farm.

'Meanwhile, the military guard has been tightened around the scene and a corridor of some eighteen miles in depth around it has been evacuated. It is known that two delegations of scientists have been escorted through the lines. While no official announcement has been made, there is good reason to believe they learned little from their visits. What the building is, who or what has engineered its construction, if you can call the inside-out process by which it grew construction, or what may be expected next are all fields of groundless speculation. There is plenty of that, naturally, but no one has yet come up with what might be called an explanation.

'The world's press wires are continuing to pile up

reams of copy, but even so there is little actual, concrete knowledge – few facts that can be listed one, two, three right down the line.

'There is little other news of any sort and perhaps it's just as well, since there is no room at the moment in the public interest for anything else but this mysterious building. As so often happens when big news breaks, all other events seem to wait for some other time to happen. The polio epidemic is rapidly subsiding; there is no major crime mews. In the world's capitals, of course, all legislative action is at a complete standstill, with the governments watching closely the developments at the building.

'There is a rising feeling at many of these capitals that the building is not of mere national concern, that decisions regarding it must be made at an international level. The attempted bombing has resulted in some argument that we, as the nation most concerned, cannot be trusted to act in a calm, dispassionate way, and that an objective world viewpoint is necessary for an intelligent handling of the situation.'

Peter got up from his bench and walked away. He'd been taken from his home three days ago, the radio had said. No wonder he was starved.

Three days – and in that time the building had grown a thousand stories high and now covered a hundred acres.

He went along, not hurrying too much now, his feet a heavy ache, his belly pinched with hunger.

He had to get back to the building – somehow he had to get back there. It was a sudden need, realized and admitted now, but the reason for it, the source of it, was not yet apparent. It was as if there had been something he had left behind and he had to go and find it. Something I left behind, he thought. What could he have left behind? Nothing but the pain and the knowledge that he walked with a dark companion and the little capsule that he carried in his pocket for the time when the pain grew too great.

He felt in his pocket and the capsule was no longer there. It had disappeared along with his wallet and his pocket knife and watch. No matter now, he thought. I no longer need the capsule.

He heard the hurrying footsteps behind him and there was an urgency about them that made him swing around.

'Peter!' Mary cried out. 'Peter, I thought I recognized you. I was hurrying to catch you.'

He stood and looked at her as if he did not quite believe it was she whom he saw.

'Where have you been?' she asked.

'Hospital,' Peter said. 'I ran away from them. But you . . .'

'We were evacuated, Peter. They came and told us that we had to leave. Some of us are at a camp down at the other end of the park. Pa is carrying on something awful and I can't blame him – having to leave right in the middle of haying and with the small grain almost ready to be cut.'

She tilted back her head and looked into his face.

'You look all worn out,' she said. 'Is it worse again?'

'It?' he asked, then realized that the neighbours must have known – that the reason for his coming to the farm must have been general knowledge, for there were no such things as secrets in a farming neighbourhood.

'I'm sorry, Peter,' Mary said. 'Terribly sorry. I shouldn't have . . .'

'It's all right,' said Peter. 'Because it's gone now, Mary. I haven't got it any more. I don't know how or why, but I've gotten rid of it in some way.'

'The hospital?' she suggested.

'The hospital had nothing to do with it. It had cleared

up before I went there. They just found out at the hospital, that is all.'

'Maybe the diagnosis was wrong.'

He shook his head. 'It wasn't wrong, Mary.'

Still, how could he be sure? How could he, or the medical world, say positively that it had been malignant cells and not something else – some strange parasite to which he had played the unsuspecting host?

'You said you ran away,' she reminded him.

'They'll be looking for me, Mary. The colonel and the major. They think I had something to do with the machine I found. They think I might have made it. They took me to the hospital to find out if I was human.'

'Of all the silly things!'

'I've got to get back to the farm,' he said. 'I simply have to get back there.'

'You can't,' she told him. 'There are soldiers everywhere.'

'I'll crawl on my belly in the ditches, if I have to. Travel at night. Sneak through the lines. Fight if I'm discovered and they try to prevent me. There is no alternative. I have to make a try.'

'You're ill,' she said, anxiously staring at his face.

He grinned at her. 'Not ill. Just hungry.'

'Come on then.' She took his arm.

He held back. 'Not to the camp. I can't have someone seeing me. In just a little while, I'll be a hunted man – if I'm not one already.'

'A restaurant, of course.'

'They took my wallet, Mary. I haven't any money.'

'I have shopping money.'

'No,' he said. 'I'll get along. There's nothing that can beat me now.'

'You really mean that, don't you?'

'It just occurred to me,' Peter admitted, confused and

yet somehow sure that what he had said was not reckless bravado, but a blunt fact.

'You're going back?'

'I have to, Mary.'

'And you think you have a chance?'

He nodded.

'Peter,' she began hesitantly.

'Yes?'

'How much bother would I be?'

'You? How do you mean? A bother in what way?'

'If I went along.'

'But you can't. There's no reason for you to.'

She lifted her chin just a little. 'There is a reason, Peter. Almost as if I were being called there. Like a bell ringing in my head – a school bell calling in the children . . .'

'Mary,' he said, 'that perfume bottle – there was a certain symbol on it, wasn't there?'

'Carved in the glass,' she told him. 'The same symbol, Peter, that was carved into the jade.'

And the same symbol, he thought, that had been on the letterheads.

'Come on,' he decided suddenly. 'You won't be any bother.'

'We'll eat first,' she said. 'We can use the shopping money.'

They walked down the path, hand in hand, like two teen-age sweethearts.

'We have lots of time,' said Peter. 'We can't start for home till dark.'

They ate at a small restaurant on an obscure street and after that went grocery shopping. They bought a loaf of bread and two rings of bologna and a slab of cheese, which took all of Mary's money, and for the change the grocer sold them an empty bottle in which to carry water. It would serve as a canteen.

They walked to the edge of the city and out through the suburbs and into the open country, not travelling fast, for there was no point in trying to go too far before night set in.

They found a stream and sat beside it, for all the world like a couple on a picnic. Mary took off her shoes and dabbled her feet in the water and the two of them felt disproportionately happy.

Night came and they started out. There was no Moon, but the sky was ablaze with stars. Although they took some tumbles and at other times wondered where they were, they kept moving on, staying off the roads, walking through the fields and pastures, skirting the farmhouses to avoid barking dogs.

It was shortly after midnight that they saw the first of the campfires and swung wide around them. From the top of a ridge, they looked down upon the camp and saw the outlines of tents and the dull shapes of the canvas-covered trucks. And, later on, they almost stumbled into an artillery outfit, but got safely away without encountering the sentries who were certain to be stationed around the perimeter of the bivouac.

Now they knew that they were inside the evacuated area, that they were moving through the outer ring of soldiers and guns which hemmed in the building.

They moved more cautiously and made slower time. When the first false light of dawn came into the east, they holed up in a dense plum thicket in the corner of a pasture.

'I'm tired,' sighed Mary. 'I wasn't tired all night or, if I was, I didn't know it – but now that we've stopped, I feel exhausted.'

'We'll eat and sleep,' Peter said.

'Sleep comes first. I'm too tired to eat.'

Peter left her and crawled through a thicket to its edge. In the growing light of morning stood the building, a great blue-misted mass that reared above the horizon like a blunted finger pointing at the sky.

'Mary!' Peter whispered. 'Mary, there it is!'

He heard her crawling through the thicket to his side.

'Peter, it's a long way off.'

'Yes, I know it is. But we are going there.'

They crouched there watching it.

'I can't see the bomb,' said Mary. 'The bomb that's hanging over it.'

'It's too far off to see.'

'Why is it us? Why are we the ones who are going back? Why are we the only ones who are not afraid?'

'I don't know,' said Peter, frowning puzzledly. 'No actual reason, that is. I'm going back because I want to – no, because I have to. You see, it was the place I chose. The dying place. Like the elephants crawling off to die where all other elephants die.'

'But you're all right now, Peter.'

'That makes no difference – or it doesn't seem to. It was where I found peace and an understanding.'

'And there were the symbols, Peter. The symbols on the bottle and the jade.'

'Let's go back,' he said. 'Someone will spot us here.'

'Our gifts were the only ones that had the symbols,' Mary persisted. 'None of the others had any of them. I asked around. There were no symbols at all on the other gifts.'

'There's no time to wonder about that. Come on.'

They crawled back to the centre of the thicket.

The Sun had risen above the horizon now and sent level shafts of light into the thicket and the early morning silence hung over them like a benediction.

'Peter,' said Mary, 'I just can't stay awake any longer. Kiss me before I go to sleep.'

He kissed her and they clung together, shut from the

world by the jagged, twisted, low-growing branches of the plum trees.

'I hear the bells,' she breathed. 'Do you hear them, too?'

Peter shook his head.

'Like school bells,' she said. 'Like bells on the first day of school – the first day you ever went.'

'You're tired,' he told her.

'I've heard them before. This is not the first time.'

He kissed her again. 'Go to sleep,' he said and she did, almost as soon as she lay down and closed her eyes.

He sat quietly beside her and his mind retreated to his own hidden depths, searching for the pain within him. But there was no pain. It was gone for ever.

The pain was gone and the incidence of polio was down and it was a crazy thing to think, but he thought it, anyhow:

Missionary!

When human missionaries went out to heathen lands, what were the first things that they did?

They preached, of course, but there were other things as well. They fought disease and they worked for sanitation and laboured to improve the welfare of the people and tried to educate them to a better way of life. And in this way they not only carried out their religious precepts, but gained the confidence of the heathen folk as well.

And if an alien missionary came to Earth, what would be among the first things that he was sure to do? Would it not be reasonable that he, too, would fight disease and try to improve the welfare of his chosen charges? Thus he would gain their confidence. Although he could not expect to gain too much at first. He could expect hostility and suspicion. Only a pitiful handful would not resent him or be afraid of him.

And if the missionary—

And if THIS missionary—

Peter fell asleep.

The roar awakened him and he sat upright, sleep entirely wiped from his mind.

The roar was still there, somewhere outside the thicket, but it was receding.

'Peter! Peter!'

'Quiet, Mary! There is something out there!'

The roar turned around and came back again, growing until it was the sound of clanking thunder and the Earth shook with the sound. It receded again.

The midday sunlight came down through the branches and made of their hiding-place a freckled spot of Sun and shade. Peter could smell the musky odour of warm soil and wilted leaf.

They crept cautiously through the thicket and when they gained its edge, where the leaves thinned out, they saw the racing tank far down the field. Its roar came to them as it tore along, bouncing and swaying to the ground's unevenness, the great snout of its cannon pugnaciously thrust out before it, like a stiff-arming football player.

A road ran clear down the field – a road that Peter was sure had not been there the night before. It was a straight road, absolutely straight, running towards the building, and it was of some metallic stuff that shimmered in the Sun.

And far off to the left was another road and to the right another, and in the distance the three roads seemed to draw together, as the rails seem to converge when one looks down a railroad track.

Other roads running at right angles cut across the three roads, intersecting them so that one gained the impression of three far-reaching ladders set tightly side by side.

The tank raced towards one of the intersecting roads, a

tank made midget by the distance, and its roar came back to them no louder than the humming of an angry bee.

It reached the road and skidded off, whipping around sideways and slewing along, as if it had hit something smooth and solid that it could not get through, as if it might have struck a soaped metallic wall. There was a moment when it tipped and almost went over, but it stayed upright and finally backed away, then swung around to come lumbering down the field, returning towards the thicket.

Halfway down the field, it pivoted around and halted, so that the gun pointed back towards the intersecting road.

The gun's muzzle moved downward and flashed and, at the intersecting road, the shell exploded with a burst of light and a puff of smoke. The concussion of the shot slapped hard against the ear.

Again and again the gun belched out its shells point-blank. A haze of smoke hung above the tank and road – and the shells still exploded at the road – this side of the road and not beyond it.

The tank clanked forward once more until it reached the road. It approached carefully this time and nudged itself along, as if it might be looking for a way to cross.

From somewhere a long distance off came the crunching sound of artillery. An entire battery of guns seemed to be firing. They fired for a while, then grudgingly quit.

The tank still nosed along the road like a dog sniffing beneath a fallen tree for a hidden rabbit.

'There's something there that's stopping them,' said Peter.

'A wall,' Mary guessed. 'An invisible wall of some sort, but one they can't get through.'

'Or shoot through, either. They tried to break through with gunfire and they didn't even dent it.'

He crouched there, watching as the tank nosed along
the road. It reached the point where the road to the left
came down to intersect the cross-road. The tank sheered
off to follow the left-hand one, bumping along with its
forward armour shoved against the unseen wall.

Boxed in, thought Peter – those roads have broken up
and boxed in all the military units. A tank in one pen and a
dozen tanks in another, a battery of artillery in another,
the motor pool in yet another. Boxed in and trapped;
penned up and useless.

And we, he wondered – are we boxed in as well?

A group of soldiers came tramping down the right-
hand road. Peter spotted them from far off, black dots
moving down the road, heading east, away from the
building. When they came closer, he saw that they carried
no guns and slogged along with the slightest semblance of
formation and he could see from the way they walked that
they were dog-tired.

He had not been aware that Mary had left his side until
she came creeping back again, ducking her head to keep
her hair from being caught in the low-hanging branches.

She sat down beside him and handed him a thick slice of
bread and a chunk of bologna. She set the bottle of water
down between them.

'It was the building,' she said, 'that built the roads.'

Peter nodded, his mouth full of bread and meat.

'They want to make it easy to get to the building,' Mary
said. 'The building wants to make it easy for people to
come and visit it.'

'The bells again?' he asked.

She smiled and said, 'The bells.'

The soldiers now had come close enough to see the tank.
They stopped and stood in the road, looking at it.

Then four of them turned off the road and walked out
into the field, heading for the tank. The others sat down
and waited.

'The wall only works one way,' said Mary.

'More likely,' Peter told her, 'it works for tanks, but doesn't work for people.'

'The building doesn't want to keep the people out.'

The soldiers crossed the field and the tank came out to meet them. It stopped and the crew crawled out of it and climbed down. The soldiers and the crew stood talking and one of the soldiers kept swinging his arms in gestures, pointing here and there.

From far away came the sound of heavy guns again.

'Some of them,' said Peter, 'still are trying to blast down the walls.'

Finally the soldiers and the tank crew walked back to the road, leaving the tank deserted in the field.

And that must be the way it was with the entire military force which had hemmed in the building. Peter told himself. The roads and walls had cut it into bits, had screened it off – and now the tanks and the big guns and the planes were just so many ineffective toys of an infant race, lying scattered in a thousand playpens.

Out on the road, the foot soldiers and the tank crew slogged eastward, retreating form the siege which had failed so ingloriously.

In their thicket, Mary and Peter sat and watched the building.

'You said they came from the stars,' said Mary. 'But why did they come here? Why did they bother with us? Why did they come at all?'

'To save us,' Peter offered slowly. 'To save us from ourselves. Or to exploit and enslave us. Or to use our planet as a military base. For any one of a hundred reasons. Maybe for a reason we couldn't understand even if they told us.'

'You don't believe those other reasons, the ones about enslaving us or using Earth as a military base. If you believed that, we wouldn't be going to the building.'

'No, I don't believe them. I don't because I had cancer and I haven't any longer. I don't because the polio began clearing up on the same day that they arrived. They're doing good for us, exactly the same as the missionaries did good among the primitive, disease-ridden people to whom they were assigned. I hope—'

He sat and stared across the field, at the trapped and deserted tank, at the shining ladder of the roads.

'I hope,' he said, 'they don't do what some of the missionaries did. I hope they don't destroy our self-respect with alien Mother Hubbards. I hope they don't save us from ringworm and condemn us to a feeling of racial inferiority. I hope they don't chop down the coconuts and hand us—'

But they know about us, he told himself. They know all there is to know. They've studied us for – how long? Squatting in a drugstore corner, masquerading as a cigarette machine. Watching us from the counter in the guise of a stamp machine.

And they wrote letters – letters to every head of state in all the world. Letters that might, when finally deciphered, explain what they were about. Or that might make certain demands. Or that might, just possibly, be no more than applications for permits to build a mission or a church or a hospital or a school.

They know us, he thought. They know, for example, that we're suckers for anything that's free, so they handed out free gifts – just like the quiz shows and contests run by radio and television and chambers of commerce, except that there was no competition and everybody won.

Throughout the afternoon, Peter and Mary watched the road and during that time small groups of soldiers had come limping down it. But now, for an hour or more, there had been no one on the road.

They started out just before dark, walking across the

field, passing through the wall-that-wasn't-there to reach the road. And they headed west along the road, going towards the purple cloud of the building that reared against the redness of the sunset.

They travelled through the night and they did not have to dodge and hide, as they had that first night, for there was no one on the road except the one lone soldier they met.

By the time they saw him, they had come far enough so that the great shaft of the building loomed halfway up the sky, a smudge of misty brightness in the bright starlight.

The soldier was sitting in the middle of the road and he'd taken off his shoes and set them neatly beside him.

'My feet are killing me,' he said by way of greeting.

So they sat down with him to keep him company and Peter took out the water-bottle and the loaf of bread and the cheese and bologna and spread them on the pavement with wrapping paper as a picnic cloth.

They ate in silence for a while and finally the soldier said, 'Well, this is the end of it.'

They did not ask the question, but waited patiently, eating bread and cheese.

'This is the end of soldiering,' the soldier told them. 'This is the end of war.'

He gestured out towards the pens fashioned by the roads and in one nearby pen were three self-propelled artillery pieces and in another was an ammunition dump and another pen held military vehicles.

'How are you going to fight a war,' the soldier asked, 'if the things back there can chop up your armies into checkerboards? A tank ain't worth a damn guarding ten acres, not when it isn't able to get out of those ten acres. A big gun ain't any good to you if you can't fire but half a mile.'

'You think they would?' asked Mary. 'Anywhere, I mean?'

'They done it here. Why not somewhere else? Why not any place that they wanted to? They stopped us. They stopped us cold and they never shed a single drop of blood. Not a casualty among us.'

He swallowed the bit of bread and cheese that was in his mouth and reached for the water-bottle. He drank, his Adam's apple bobbing up and down.

'I'm coming back,' he said. 'I'm going out and get my girl and we both are coming back. The things in that building maybe need some help and I'm going to help them if there's a way of doing it. And if they don't need no help, why, then I'm going to figure out some way to let them know I'm thankful that they came.'

'Things? You saw some things?'

The soldier stared at Peter. 'No, I never saw anything at all.'

'But this business of going out to get your girl and both of you coming back? How did you get that idea? Why not go back right now with us?'

'It wouldn't be right,' the soldier protested. 'Or it doesn't seem just right. I got to see her first and tell her how I feel. Besides, I got a present for her.'

'She'll be glad to see you,' Mary told him softly. 'She'll like the present.'

'She sure will.' The soldier grinned proudly. 'It was something that she wanted.'

He reached in his pocket and took out a leather box. Fumbling with the catch, he snapped it open. The starlight blazed softly on the necklace that lay inside the box.

Mary reached out her hand. 'May I?' she asked.

'Sure,' the soldier said. 'I want you to take a look at it. You'd know if a girl would like it.'

Mary lifted if from the box and held it in her hand, a stream of starlit fire.

'Diamonds?' asked Peter.

'I don't know,' the soldier said. 'Might be. It looks real expensive. There's a pendant, sort of, at the bottom of it, of green stone that doesn't sparkle much, but—'

'Peter,' Mary interrupted, 'have you got a match?'

The soldier dipped his hand into a pocket. 'I got a lighter, Miss. That thing gave me a lighter. A beaut!'

He snapped it open and the blaze flamed out. Mary held the pendant close.

'It's the symbol,' she said. 'Just like on my bottle of perfume.'

'That carving?' asked the soldier, pointing. 'It's on the lighter, too.'

'Something gave you this?' Peter urgently wanted to know.

'A box. Except that it really was more than a box. I reached down to put my hand on it and it coughed up a lighter and when it did, I thought of Louise and the lighter she had given me. I'd lost it and I felt bad about it, and here was one just like it except for the carving on the side. And when I thought of Louise, the box made a funny noise and out popped the box with the necklace in it.'

The soldier leaned forward, his young face solemn in the glow from the lighter's flame.

'You know what I think?' he said. 'I think that box was one of them. There are stories, but you can't believe everything you hear . . .'

He looked from one to the other of them. 'You don't laugh at me,' he remarked wonderingly.

Peter shook his head. 'That's about the last thing we'd do, Soldier.'

Mary handed back the necklace and the lighter. The soldier put them in his pocket and began putting on his shoes.

'I got to get on,' he said. 'Thanks for the chow.'

'We'll be seeing you,' said Peter.

'I hope so.'

'I know we will,' Mary stated positively.

They watched him trudge away, then walked on in the other direction.

Mary said to Peter, 'The symbol is the mark of them. The ones who get the symbol are the ones who will go back. It's a passport, a seal of approval.'

'Or,' Peter amended, 'the brand of ownership.'

'They'd be looking for certain kinds of people. They wouldn't want anybody who was afraid of them. They'd want people who had some faith in them.'

'What do they want us for?' Peter fretted. 'That's what bothers me. What use can we be to them? The soldier wants to help them, but they don't need help from us. They don't need help from anyone.'

'We've never seen one of them,' said Mary. 'Unless the box was one of them.'

And the cigarette machines, thought Peter. The cigarette machines and God knows what else.

'And yet,' said Mary, 'they know about us. They've watched us and studied us. They know us inside out. They can reach deep within us and know what each of us might want and then give it to us. A rod and reel for Johnny and a piece of jade for you. And the rod and reel were a *human* rod and reel and the jade was Earth jade. They even know about the soldier's girl. They knew she would like a shiny necklace and they knew she was the kind of person that they wanted to come back again and . . .'

'The Saucers,' Peter said. 'I wonder if it was the Saucers, after all, watching us for years, learning all about us.'

How many years would it take, he wondered, from a standing start, to learn all there was to know about the human race? For it would be from a standing start; to them, all of humanity would have been a complex alien race and they would have had to feel their way along, learning one fact here and another there. And they would make mistakes; at times their deductions would be wrong, and that would set them back.

'I don't know,' said Peter. 'I can't figure it out at all.'

They walked down the shiny metal road that glimmered in the starlight, with the building growing from a misty phantom to a gigantic wall that rose against the sky to blot out the stars. A thousand stories high and covering more than a hundred acres, it was a structure that craned your head and set your neck to aching and made your brain spin with its glory and its majesty.

And even when you drew near it, you could not see the dropped and cradled bomb, resting in the emptiness above it, for the bomb was too far away for seeing.

But you could see the little cubicles sliced off by the roads and, within the cubicles, the destructive toys of a violent race, deserted now, just idle hunks of fashioned metal.

They came at last, just before dawn, to the great stairs that ran up to the central door. As they moved across the flat stone approach to the stairs, they felt the hush and the deepness of the peace that lay in the building's shadow.

Hand in hand, they went up the stairs and came to the great bronze door and there they stopped. Turning around, they looked back in silence.

The roads spun out like wheel spokes from the building's hub as far as they could see, and the crossing roads ran in concentric circles so that it seemed they stood in the centre of a spider's web.

Deserted farmhouses, with their groups of buildings – barns, granaries, garages, silos, hog pens, machine sheds – stood in the sectors marked off by the roads, and in other sectors lay the machines of war, fit now for little more than birds' nests or a hiding-place for rabbits. Bird songs came trilling up from the pastures and the fields and you could smell the freshness and the coolness of the countryside.

'It's good,' said Mary. 'It's our country, Peter.'

'It was our country,' Peter corrected her. 'Nothing will ever be quite the same again.'

'You aren't afraid, Peter?'

'Not a bit. Just baffled.'

'But you seemed so sure before.'

'I still am sure,' he said. 'Emotionally, I am as sure as ever that everything's all right.'

'Of course everything's all right. There was a polio epidemic and now it has died out. An army has been routed without a single death. An atomic bomb was caught and halted before it could go off. Can't you see, Peter, they're already making this a better world. Cancer and polio gone – two things that Man had fought for years and was far from conquering. War stopped, disease stopped, atomic bombs stopped – things we couldn't solve for ourselves that were solved for us.'

'I know all that,' said Peter. 'They'll undoubtedly also put an end to crime and graft and violence and every-thing else that has been tormenting and degrading man-kind since it climbed down out of the trees.'

'What more do you want?'

'Nothing more, I guess – it's just that it's circumstantial. It's not real evidence. All that we know, or think we know, we've learned from inference. We have no proof – no actual, solid proof.'

'We have faith. We must have faith. If you can't believe in someone or something that wipes out disease and war, what can you believe in?'

'That's what bothers me.'

'The world is built on faith,' said Mary. 'Faith in God and in ourselves and in the decency of mankind.'

'You're wonderful,' exclaimed Peter.

He caught her tight and kissed her and she clung against him and when finally they let each other go, the great bronze door was opening.

Silently, they walked across the threshold with arms around each other, into a foyer that arched high overhead. There were murals on the high arched ceiling, and others panelled in the walls, and four great flights of stairs led upward.

But the stairways were roped off by heavy velvet cords. Another cord, hooked into gleaming standards, and signs with pointing arrows showed them which way to go.

Obediently, walking in the hush that came close to reverence, they went across the foyer to the single open door.

They stepped into a large room, with great, tall, slender windows that let in the morning sunlight, and it fell across the satin newness of the blackboards, the big-armed class chairs, the heavy reading tables, case after case of books, and the lectern on the lecture platform.

They stood and looked at it and Mary said to Peter: 'I was right. They were school bells, after all. We've come to school, Peter. The first day we ever went to school.'

'Kindergarten,' Peter said, and his voice choked as he pronounced the word.

It was just right, he thought, so humanly right: the sunlight and the shadow, the rich bindings of the books, the dark patina of the wood the heavy silence over everything. It was an Earthly classroom in the most scholarly tradition. It was Cambridge and Oxford and the Sorbonne and an Eastern ivy college all rolled into one.

The aliens hadn't missed a bet – not a single bet.

'I have to go,' said Mary. 'You wait right here for me.'

'I'll wait right here,' he promised.

He watched her cross the room and open a door. Through it, he saw a corridor that went on for what seemed miles and miles. Then she shut the door and he was alone.

He stood there for a moment, then swung swiftly around. Almost running across the foyer, he reached the great bronze door. But there was no door, or none that he could see. There was not even a crack where a door should be. He went over the wall inch by inch and he found no door.

He turned away from the wall and stood in the foyer, naked of soul, and felt the vast emptiness of the building thunder in his brain.

Up there, he thought, up there for a thousand stories, the building stretched into the sky. And down here was kindergarten and up on the second floor, no doubt, first grade, and you'd go up and up and what would be the end – and the purpose of that end?

When did you graduate?

Or did you ever graduate?

And when you graduated, what would you be?

What would you be? he asked.

Would you be human still?

They would be coming to school for days, the ones who had been picked, the ones who had passed the strange entrance examination that was necessary to attend this school. They'd come down the metal roads and climb the steps and the great bronze door would open and they would enter. And others would come, too, out of curiosity, but if they did not have the symbol, the doors would not open for them.

And those who did come in, when and if they felt the urge to flee, would find there were no doors.

He went back into the classroom and stood where he had stood before.

Those books, he wondered. What was in them? In just a little while, he'd have the courage to pick one out and see. And the lectern? What would stand behind the lectern?

What, not *who*.

The door opened and Mary came across the room to him.

'There are apartments out there,' she said. 'The cutest apartments you have ever seen. And one of them has our names on it and there are others that have other names and some that have no names at all. There are other people coming, Peter. We were just a little early. We were the ones who started first. We got here before the school bell rang.'

Peter nodded. 'Let's sit down and wait,' he said.

Side by side, they sat down, waiting for the Teacher.